THE DIARY OF A PROVINCIAL LADY

E. M. Delafield

Gently malicious, the Provincial Lady is anything but provincial in outlook, and the enjoyment she gets out of the mishaps of pre-war existence is very happily reflected in the pages of this good-humoured, high-spirited book. It is all very true to middle-class life as it used to be—the recalcitrant cook, the callous children, the patronizing squiress, and the village characters who are seen without sentiment.

'*A cheerful holiday book*', the Times Literary Supplement called it on its first appearance in the Thirties. This it certainly still is today.

E. M. Delafield

THE DIARY OF A PROVINCIAL LADY

With Illustrations
by
ARTHUR WATTS

HOWARD BAKER
LONDON

Originally published in Great Britain 1930
First Howard Baker edition 1969
This edition 1978

ISBN: 0 7030 0153 1

A HOWARD BAKER BOOK

Published by Howard Baker Press Ltd.,
27a Arterberry Road, Wimbledon, London SW20

Printed in Great Britain by A. Wheaton & Co. Ltd., Exeter

DIARY OF A PROVINCIAL LADY

November 7th.—Plant the indoor bulbs. Just as I am in the middle of them, Lady Boxe calls. I say, untruthfully, how nice to see her, and beg her to sit down while I just finish the bulbs. Lady B. makes determined attempt to sit down in armchair where I have already placed two bulb-bowls and the bag of charcoal, is headed off just in time, and takes the sofa.

Do I know, she asks, how very late it is for indoor bulbs? September, really, or even October, is the time. Do I know that the only really reliable firm for hyacinths is Somebody of Haarlem? Cannot catch the name of the firm, which is Dutch, but reply Yes, I do know, but think it my duty to buy Empire products. Feel at the time, and still think, that this is an excellent reply. Unfortunately Vicky comes into the drawing-room later and says: "O Mummie, are those the bulbs we got at Woolworths?"

Lady B. stays to tea. (*Mem.*: Bread-and-butter too thick. Speak to Ethel.) We talk some more about bulbs, the Dutch School of Painting, our Vicar's wife, sciatica, and *All Quiet on the Western Front*.

(Query: Is it possible to cultivate the art of conversation when living in the country all the year round?)

Lady B. enquires after the children. Tell her that Robin—whom I refer to in a detached way as "the boy" so that she shan't think I am foolish about him—is getting on fairly well at school, and that Mademoiselle says Vicky is starting a cold.

Do I realise, says Lady B., that the Cold Habit is entirely unnecessary, and can be avoided by giving the child a nasal douche of salt-and-water every morning before breakfast? Think of several rather tart and witty rejoinders to this, but unfortunately not until Lady B.'s Bentley has taken her away.

Finish the bulbs and put them in the cellar. Feel that after all cellar is probably draughty, change my mind, and take them all up to the attic.

Cook says something is wrong with the range.

November 8th.—Robert has looked at the range and says nothing wrong whatever. Makes unoriginal suggestion about pulling out dampers. Cook very angry, and will probably give notice. Try to propitiate her by saying that we are going to Bournemouth for Robin's half-term, and that will give the household a rest. Cook replies austerely that they will take the opportunity to do some extra cleaning. Wish I could believe this was true.

Preparations for Bournemouth rather marred by discovering that Robert, in bringing down the suit-cases from the attic, has broken three of the bulb-bowls. Says he understood that I had put them in the cellar, and so wasn't expecting them.

November 11th.—Bournemouth. Find that history, as usual, repeats itself. Same hotel, same frenzied scurry round the school to find Robin, same collection of parents, most of them also staying at the hotel. Discover strong tendency to exchange with fellow-parents exactly the same remarks as last year, and the year before that. Speak of this to Robert, who returns no answer. Perhaps he is afraid of repeating himself? This suggests Query: Does Robert, perhaps, take in what I say even when he makes no reply?

Find Robin looking thin, and speak to Matron who says brightly, Oh no, she thinks on the whole he's put *on* weight this term, and then begins to talk about the New Buildings. (Query: Why do all schools have to run up New Buildings about once in every six months?)

Take Robin out. He eats several meals, and a good many sweets. He produces a friend, and we take both to Corfe Castle. The boys climb, Robert smokes in silence, and I sit about on stones. Overhear a woman remark, as she gazes up at half a tower, that has withstood several centuries, that This looks *fragile*—which strikes me as a singular choice of adjective. Same woman, climbing over a block of solid masonry, points out that This has evidently fallen off somewhere.

Take the boys back to the hotel for dinner. Robin says, whilst the friend is out of hearing: "It's been nice for us, taking out Williams, hasn't it?" Hastily express appreciation of this privilege.

Robert takes the boys back after dinner, and I sit in hotel lounge with several other mothers and we all talk about our boys in tones of disparagement, and about one another's boys with great enthusiasm.

Am asked what I think of *Harriet Hume* but am unable to say, as I have not read it. Have a depressed feeling that this is going to be another case of *Orlando* about which was perfectly able to talk most intelligently until I read it, and found myself unfortunately unable to understand any of it.

Robert comes up very late and says he must have dropped asleep over the *Times*. (Query: Why come to Bournemouth to do this?)

Postcard by the last post from Lady B. to ask if I have remembered that there is a Committee Meeting of the Women's Institute on the 14th. Should not dream of answering this.

November 12th.—Home yesterday and am struck, as so often before, by immense accumulation of domestic disasters that always await one after any absence. Trouble with kitchen range has resulted in no hot water, also Cook says the mutton has *gone*, and will I speak to the butcher, there being no excuse weather like this. Vicky's cold, unlike the mutton, hasn't gone. Mademoiselle says, "Ah, cette petite! Elle ne sera peut-être pas longtemps pour ce bas monde, madame." Hope that this is only her Latin way of dramatising the situation.

Robert reads the *Times* after dinner, and goes to sleep.

November 13*th.*—Interesting, but disconcerting, train of thought started by prolonged discussion with Vicky as to the existence or otherwise of a locality which she refers to throughout as H. E. L. Am determined to be a modern parent, and assure her that there is not, never has been, and never could be, such a place. Vicky maintains that there *is*, and refers me to the Bible. I become more modern than ever, and tell her that theories of eternal punishment were invented to frighten people. Vicky replies indignantly that they don't frighten her in the least, she *likes* to think about H. E. L. Feel that deadlock has been reached, and can only leave her to her singular method of enjoying herself.

(Query: Are modern children going to revolt against being modern, and if so, what form will reaction of modern parents take?)

Much worried by letter from the Bank to say that my account is overdrawn to the extent of Eight Pounds, four shillings, and fourpence. Cannot understand this, as was convinced that I still had credit balance of Two Pounds, seven shillings, and sixpence. Annoyed to find that my accounts, contents of cash-box, and counterfoils in cheque-book, do not tally. (*Mem.*: Find envelope on which I jotted down Bournemouth expenses, also little piece of paper (probably last leaf of grocer's book) with note about cash payment to sweep. This may clear things up.)

Take a look at bulb-bowls on returning suit-case to attic, and am inclined to think it looks as though the cat had been up here. If so, this will be the last straw. Shall tell Lady Boxe that I sent all my bulbs to a sick friend in a nursing-home.

November 14*th.*—Arrival of Book of the Month choice, and am disappointed. History of a place I am not interested in, by an author I do not like. Put it back into its wrapper again and make fresh choice from Recommended List. Find, on reading small literary bulletin enclosed with book, that exactly this course of procedure has been anticipated, and that it is described as being "the mistake of a lifetime". Am much annoyed, although not so much at having made (possibly) mistake of a lifetime, as at depressing thought of our all being so much alike that intelligent writers can apparently predict our behaviour with perfect accuracy.

Decide not to mention any of this to Lady B., always so tiresomely superior about Book of the Month as it is, taking up attitude that she does not require to be told what to read. (Should like to think of good repartee to this.)

Letter by second post from my dear old school-friend Cissie Crabbe, asking if she may come here for two nights or so on her way to Norwich. (Query: Why Norwich? Am surprised to realise that anybody ever goes to, lives at, or comes from, Norwich, but quite see that this is unreasonable of me. Remind myself how very little one knows of the England one lives in, which vaguely suggests a quotation. This, however, does not materialise.)

Many years since we last met, writes Cissie, and she expects we have both *changed* a good deal. *P.S.* Do I remember the dear old *pond*, and the day of the Spanish Arrowroot. Can recall, after some thought, dear old pond, at bottom of Cissie's father's garden, but am completely baffled by Spanish Arrowroot. (Query: Could this be one of the Sherlock Holmes stories? Sounds like it.)

Reply that we shall be delighted to see her, and what a lot we shall have to talk about, after all these years! (This, I find on reflection, is not true, but cannot re-write letter on that account.) Ignore Spanish Arrowroot altogether.

Robert, when I tell him about dear old school-friend's impending arrival, does not seem pleased. Asks what we are expected to *do* with her. I suggest showing her the garden, and remember too late that this is hardly the right time of the year. At any rate, I say, it will be nice to talk over old times—(which reminds me of the Spanish Arrowroot reference still unfathomed).

Speak to Ethel about the spare room, and am much annoyed to find that one blue candlestick has been broken, and the bedside rug has gone to the cleaners, and cannot be retrieved in time. Take away bedside rug from Robert's dressing-room, and put it in spare room instead, hoping he will not notice its absence.

November 15th.—Robert *does* notice absence of rug, and says he must have it back again. Return it to dressing-room and take small and inferior dyed mat from the night-nursery to put in spare room. Mademoiselle is hurt about this and says to Vicky, who repeats it to me, that in this country she finds herself treated like a worm.

November 17*th*.—Dear old school-friend Cissie Crabbe due by the three o'clock train. On telling Robert this, he says it is most inconvenient to meet her, owing to Vestry Meeting, but eventually agrees to abandon Vestry Meeting. Am touched. Unfortunately, just after he has started, telegram arrives to say that dear old school-friend has missed the connection and will not arrive until seven o'clock. This means putting off dinner till eight, which Cook won't like. Cannot send message to kitchen by Ethel, as it is her afternoon out, so am obliged to tell Cook myself. She is not pleased. Robert returns from station, not pleased either. Mademoiselle, quite inexplicably, says, "Il ne manquait que ça!" (This comment wholly unjustifiable, as non-appearance of Cissie Crabbe cannot concern her in any way. Have often thought that the French are tactless.)

Ethel returns, ten minutes late, and says Shall she light fire in spare room? I say No, it is not cold enough—but really mean that

"ROBERT READS THE *TIMES*."

COOK.

Cissie is no longer, in my opinion, deserving of luxuries. Subsequently feel this to be unworthy attitude, and light fire myself. It smokes.

Robert calls up to know What is that Smoke? I call down that It is Nothing. Robert comes up and opens the window and shuts the door and says It will Go all right Now. Do not like to point out that the open window will make the room cold.

Play Ludo with Vicky in drawing-room.

Robert reads the *Times* and goes to sleep, but wakes in time to make second expedition to the station. Thankful to say that this time he returns with Cissie Crabbe, who has put on weight, and says several times that she supposes we have both *changed* a good deal, which I consider unnecessary.

Take her upstairs—spare room like an ice-house, owing to open window, and fire still smoking, though less—She says room is delightful, and I leave her, begging her to ask for anything she wants—(*Mem.*: tell Ethel she *must* answer spare room bell if it rings— Hope it won't.)

Ask Robert while dressing for dinner what he thinks of Cissie. He says he has not known her long enough to judge. Ask if he thinks her good-looking. He says he has not thought about it. Ask what they talked about on the way from the station. He says he does not remember.

November 19th.—Last two days very, very trying, owing to quite unexpected discovery that Cissie Crabbe is strictly on a diet. This causes Robert to take a dislike to her. Utter impossibility of obtaining lentils *or* lemons at short notice makes housekeeping unduly difficult. Mademoiselle in the middle of lunch insists on discussing diet question, and several times exclaims: "Ah, mon doux St. Joseph!" which I consider profane, and beg her never to repeat.

Consult Cissie about the bulbs, which look very much as if the mice had been at

them. She says: Unlimited Watering, and
tells me about her own bulbs at Norwich.
Am discouraged.

Administer Unlimited Water to the
bulbs (some of which goes through the
attic floor on to the landing below), and
move half of them down to the cellar, as
Cissie Crabbe says attic is airless.

Our Vicar's wife calls this afternoon.
Says she once knew someone who had relations living near Norwich, but cannot remember their name. Cissie Crabbe replies
that very likely if we knew their name we
might find she'd heard of them, or even
met them. We agree that the world is a small
place. Talk about the Riviera, the new
waist-line, choir-practice, the servant question, and Ramsay MacDonald.

November 22nd.—Cissie Crabbe leaves.
Begs me in the kindest way to stay with her
in Norwich (where she has already told me
that she lives in a bed-sitting-room with
two cats, and cooks her own lentils on a gas-

ring). I say Yes, I should love to. We part effusively.

Spend entire morning writing the letters I have had to leave unanswered during Cissie's visit.

Invitation from Lady Boxe to us to dine and meet distinguished literary friends staying with her, one of whom is the author of *Symphony in Three Sexes*. Hesitate to write back and say that I have never heard of *Symphony in Three Sexes*, so merely accept. Ask for *Symphony in Three Sexes* at the library, although doubtfully. Doubt more than justified by tone in which Mr. Jones replies that it is not in stock, and never has been.

Ask Robert whether he thinks I had better wear my Blue or my Black-and-gold at Lady B.'s. He says that either will do. Ask if he can remember which one I wore last time. He cannot. Mademoiselle says it was the Blue, and offers to make slight alterations to Black-and-gold which will, she says, render it unrecognisable. I accept, and she cuts large pieces out of the back of it. I say: "Pas trop décolletée," and she replies intelligently: "Je comprends, Madame ne désire pas se voir nue au salon."

(Query: Have not the French sometimes a very strange way of expressing themselves, and will this react unfavourably on Vicky?)

Tell Robert about the distinguished literary friends, but do not mention *Symphony in Three Sexes*. He makes no answer.

Have absolutely decided that if Lady B. should introduce us to distinguished literary friends, or anyone else, as Our Agent, and Our Agent's Wife, I shall at once leave the house.

Tell Robert this. He says nothing. (*Mem.*: Put evening shoes out of window to see if fresh air will remove smell of petrol.)

November 25th.—Go and get hair cut and have manicure in the morning, in honour of Lady B.'s dinner party. Should like new pair of evening stockings, but depressing communication from Bank, still maintaining that I am overdrawn, prevents this, also rather unpleasantly worded letter from Messrs. Frippy and Coleman requesting payment of overdue account by return of post. Think better not to mention this to Robert, as bill for coke arrived yesterday, also reminder that Rates are much overdue, therefore write civilly to Messrs. F. and C. to the effect that cheque follows in a few days. (Hope they may think I have temporarily mislaid cheque-book.)

Black-and-gold as rearranged by Mademoiselle very satisfactory, but am obliged to do my hair five times owing to wave having been badly set. Robert unfortunately comes in just as I am using bran-new and expensive lip-stick, and objects strongly to result.

(Query: If Robert could be induced to go to London rather oftener, would he perhaps take broader view of these things?)

Am convinced we are going to be late, as Robert has trouble in getting car to start, but he refuses to be agitated. Am bound to add that subsequent events justify this attitude, as we arrive before anybody else, also before Lady B. is down. Count at least a dozen Roman hyacinths growing in bowls all over the drawing-room. (Probably grown by one of the gardeners, whatever Lady B. may say. Resolve not to comment on them in any way, but am conscious that this is slightly ungenerous.)

Lady B. comes down wearing silver lace frock that nearly touches the floor all round, and has new waist-line. This may or not be becoming, but has effect of making everybody else's frock look out-of-date.

Nine other people present besides ourselves, most of them staying in house. Nobody is introduced. Decide that a lady in what looks like blue tapestry is probably responsible for *Symphony in Three Sexes*.

Just as dinner is announced Lady B. murmurs to me: "I've put you next to Sir William. He's interested in *water-supplies*, you know, and I thought you'd like to talk to him about local conditions."

Find, to my surprise, that Sir W. and I embark almost at once on the subject of Birth Control. Why or how this topic presents itself cannot say at all, but greatly prefer it to water-supplies. On the other side of the table, Robert is sitting next to *Symphony in Three Sexes*. Hope he is enjoying himself.

Conversation becomes general. Everybody (except Robert) talks about books. We all say (*a*) that we have read *The Good Companions*, (*b*) that it is a very *long* book, (*c*) that it was chosen by the Book of the Month Club in America and must be having immense sales, and (*d*) that American sales are What Really Count. We then turn to *High Wind in Jamaica* and say (*a*) that it is quite a short book, (*b*) that we hated—or, alternatively, adored—it, and (*c*) that it Really *Is* exactly *Like* Children. A small minority here surges into being, and maintains No, they Cannot Believe that

any children in the World wouldn't ever
have *noticed* that John wasn't there any
more. They can swallow everything else,
they say, but not *that*. Discussion very active
indeed. I talk to pale young man with horn-
rimmed glasses, sitting at my left-hand,
about Jamaica, where neither of us has ever
been. This leads—but cannot say how—to
stag-hunting, and eventually to homeo-
pathy. (*Mem.*: Interesting, if time per-
mitted, to trace train of thought leading on
from one topic to another. Second, and most
disquieting idea: perhaps no such train of
thought exists.) Just as we reach interchange
of opinions about growing cucumbers under
glass, Lady B. gets up.

Go into the drawing-room, and all exclaim how nice it is to see the fire. Room
very cold. (Query: Is this good for the
bulbs?) Lady in blue tapestry takes down
her hair, which she says she is growing, and
puts it up again. We all begin to talk about
hair. Depressed to find that everybody in
the world, except apparently myself, has

grown, or is growing, long hair again. Lady B. says that Nowadays, there Isn't a Shingled Head to be seen *anywhere*, either in London, Paris, or New York. Nonsense.

Discover, in the course of the evening, that the blue tapestry has nothing whatever to do with literature, but is a Government Sanitary Inspector, and that *Symphony in Three Sexes* was written by pale young man with glasses. Lady B. says, Did I get him on to the subject of *perversion*, as he is always so amusing about it? I reply evasively.

Men come in, and all herded into billiard room (just as drawing-room seems to be getting slightly warmer) where Lady B. inaugurates unpleasant game of skill with billiard balls, involving possession of a Straight Eye, which most of us do not possess. Robert does well at this. Am thrilled, and feel it to be more satisfactory way of acquiring distinction than even authorship of *Symphony in Three Sexes*.

Congratulate Robert on the way home, but he makes no reply.

November 26th.—Robert says at breakfast that he thinks we are no longer young enough for late nights.

Frippy and Coleman regret that they can no longer allow account to stand over, but must request favour of a cheque by return, or will be compelled, with utmost regret, to take Further Steps. Have written to Bank to transfer Six Pounds, thirteen shillings, and tenpence from Deposit Account to Current. (This leaves Three Pounds, seven shillings, and twopence, to keep Deposit Account open.) Decide to put off paying milk book till next month, and to let cleaners have something on account instead of full settlement. This enables me to send F. and C. cheque, post-dated Dec. 1st, when allowance becomes due. Financial instability very trying.

November 28th.—Receipt from F. and C.

assuring me of attention to my future wishes—but evidently far from realising magnitude of effort involved in setting myself straight with them.

December 1st.—Cable from dear Rose saying she lands at Tilbury on 10th. Cable back welcome, and will meet her Tilbury, 10th. Tell Vicky that her godmother, my dearest friend, is returning home after three years in America. Vicky says: "Oh, will she have a present for me?" Am disgusted with her mercenary attitude and complain to Mademoiselle, who replies: "Si la Sainte Vierge revenait sur la terre, madame, ce serait notre petite Vicky." Do not at all agree with this. Moreover, in other moods Mademoiselle first person to refer to Vicky as "ce petit démon enragé".

(Query: Are the Latin races always as sincere as one would wish them to be?)

December 3rd.—Radio from dear Rose, landing Plymouth 8th after all. Send return message, renewed welcomes, and will meet her Plymouth.

Robert adopts unsympathetic attitude and says This is Waste of Time and Money. Do not know if he means cables, or journey to meet ship, but feel sure better not to enquire. Shall go to Plymouth on 7th. (*Mem.*: Pay grocer's book before I go, and tell him last lot of gingernuts were soft. Find out first if Ethel kept tin properly shut.)

December 8th.—Plymouth. Arrived last night, terrific storm, ship delayed. Much distressed at thought of Rose, probably suffering severe sea-sickness. Wind howls round hotel, which shakes, rain lashes against window-pane all night. Do not like my room and have unpleasant idea that someone may have committed a murder in it. Mysterious door in corner which I feel conceals a corpse. Remember all the stories I have read to this effect, and cannot sleep. Finally open mysterious door and find large cupboard, but no corpse. Go back to bed again.

Storm worse than ever in the morning, am still more distressed at thought of Rose, who will probably have to be carried off ship in state of collapse.

Go round to Shipping Office and am told to be on docks at ten o'clock. Having had previous experience of this, take fur coat, camp-stool, and copy of *American Tragedy* as being longest book I can find, and camp myself on docks. Rain stops. Other people turn up and look enviously at camp-stool. Very old lady in black totters up and down till I feel guilty, and offer to give up camp-stool to her. She replies: "Thank you, thank you, but my Daimler is outside, and I can sit in that when I wish to do so."

Return to *American Tragedy* feeling discouraged.

Find *American Tragedy* a little oppressive, but read on and on for about two hours when policeman informs me that tender is about to start for ship, if I wish to go on board. Remove self, camp-stool, and

American Tragedy to tender. Read for forty minutes. (*Mem.*: Ask Rose if American life is really like that.)

Very, very unpleasant half-hour follows. Camp-stool shows tendency to slide about all over the place, and am obliged to abandon *American Tragedy* for the time being.

Numbers of men of seafaring aspect walk about and look at me. One of them asks Am I a good sailor? No, I am not. Presently ship appears, apparently suddenly rising up from the middle of the waves, and ropes are dangled in every direction. Just as I catch sight of Rose, tender is carried away from ship's side by colossal waves.

Consoled by reflection that Rose is evidently not going to require carrying on shore, but presently begin to feel that boot, as they say, may be on the other leg.

More waves, more ropes, and tremendous general activity.

I return to camp-stool, but have no strength left to cope with *American Tragedy*.

A man in oilskins tells me I am In the Way there, Miss.

Remove myself, camp-stool, and *American Tragedy* to another corner. A man in sea-boots says that If I stay there, I may get Badly Knocked About.

Renewed déménagement of self, camp-stool, *American Tragedy*. Am slightly comforted by having been called "Miss".

Catch glimpse of Rose from strange angles as tender heaves up and down. Gangway eventually materialises, and self, camp-stool, and *American Tragedy* achieve the ship. Realise too late that camp-stool and *American Tragedy* might equally well have remained where they were.

Dear Rose most appreciative of effort involved by coming to meet her, but declares herself perfectly good sailor, and slept all through last night's storm. Try hard not to feel unjustly injured about this.

December 9th.—Rose staying here two days before going on to London. Says All

American houses are Always Warm, which annoys Robert. He says in return that All American houses are Grossly Overheated and Entirely Airless. Impossible not to feel that this would carry more weight if Robert had ever been to America. Rose also very insistent about efficiency of American Telephone Service, and inclined to ask for glasses of cold water at breakfast time—which Robert does not approve of.

Otherwise dear Rose entirely unchanged and offers to put me up in her West-End flat as often as I like to come to London. Accept gratefully. (*N.B.* How very different to old school-friend Cissie Crabbe, with bed-sitting-room and gas-ring in Norwich! But should not like to think myself in any way a snob.)

On Rose's advice, bring bulb-bowls up from cellar and put them in drawing-room. Several of them perfectly visible, but somehow do not look entirely healthy. Rose thinks too much watering. If so, Cissie Crabbe entirely to blame. (*Mem.*:

Either move bulb-bowls upstairs, or tell Ethel to show Lady Boxe into morning-room, if she calls. Cannot possibly enter into further discussion with her concerning bulbs.)

December 10th.—Robert, this morning, complains of insufficient breakfast. Cannot feel that porridge, scrambled eggs, toast, marmalade, scones, brown bread, and coffee give adequate grounds for this, but admit that porridge is slightly burnt. How impossible ever to encounter burnt porridge without vivid recollections of Jane Eyre at Lowood School, say I parenthetically! This literary allusion not a success. Robert suggests ringing for Cook, and have greatest difficulty in persuading him that this course utterly disastrous.

Eventually go myself to kitchen, in ordinary course of events, and approach subject of burnt porridge circuitously and with utmost care. Cook replies, as I expected, with expressions of astonishment and incredulity, coupled with assurances that kitchen range is again at fault. She also says that new double-saucepan, fish-kettle, and nursery tea-cups are urgently required. Make enquiries regarding recently purchased nursery tea-set and am shown one handle without cup, saucer in three pieces, and cup from which large semicircle has apparently been bitten. Feel that Mademoiselle will be hurt if I pursue enquiries further. (Note: Extreme sensibility of the French sometimes makes them difficult to deal with.)

Read Life and Letters of distinguished woman recently dead, and am struck, as so often, by difference between her correspondence and that of less distinguished women. Immense and affectionate letters from celebrities on every other page, epigrammatic notes from literary and political acquaintances, poetical assurances of affection and admiration from husband, and even infant children. Try to imagine Robert writing in similar strain in the (improbable) event of my attaining celebrity, but fail. Dear Vicky equally unlikely to commit her feelings (if any) to paper.

Robin's letter arrives by second post, and am delighted to have it as ever, but cannot feel that laconic information about boy—unknown to me—called Baggs, having been swished, and Mr. Gompshaw, visiting master, being kept away by Sore Throat—is on anything like equal footing with lengthy and picturesque epistles received almost daily by subject of biography, whenever absent from home.

Remainder of mail consists of one bill from chemist—(*Mem.*: Ask Mademoiselle why *two* tubes of Gibbs' Toothpaste within ten days)—illiterate postcard from piano-tuner, announcing visit to-morrow, and circular concerning True Temperance.

Inequalities of Fate very curious. Should like, on this account, to believe in Re-incarnation. Spend some time picturing to myself completely renovated state of affairs, with, amongst other improvements, total reversal of relative positions of Lady B. and myself.

(Query: Is thought on abstract questions ever a waste of time?)

December 11*th.*—Robert, still harping on topic of yesterday's breakfast, says suddenly Why Not a Ham? to which I reply austerely that a ham is on order, but will not appear until arrival of R.'s brother William and his wife, for Christmas visit. Robert, with every manifestation of horror, says Are William and Angela coming to us for *Christmas?* This attitude absurd, as invitation was given months ago, at Robert's own suggestion.

(Query here becomes unavoidable: Does not a misplaced optimism exist, common to all mankind, leading on to false conviction that social engagements, if dated sufficiently far ahead, will never really materialise?)

Vicky and Mademoiselle return from walk with small white-and-yellow kitten, alleged by them homeless and starving.

Vicky fetches milk, and becomes excited. Agree that kitten shall stay "for to-night" but feel that this is weak.

(*Mem.*: Remind Vicky to-morrow that Daddy does not like cats.) Mademoiselle becomes very French, on subject of cats generally, and am obliged to check her. She is *blessée*, and all three retire to schoolroom.

December 12*th.*—Robert says out of the question to keep stray kitten. Existing kitchen cat more than enough. Gradually modifies this attitude under Vicky's pleadings. All now depends on whether kitten is male or female. Vicky and Mademoiselle declare this is known to them, and kitten already christened Napoleon. Find myself unable to enter into discussion on the point in French. The gardener takes opposite view to Vicky's and Mademoiselle's. They thereupon re-christen the kitten, seen playing with an old tennis ball, as Helen Wills.

Robert's attention, perhaps fortunately, diverted by mysterious trouble with the

MADEMOISELLE.

THE RECTOR.

water-supply. He says The Ram has Stopped. (This sounds to me Biblical.)

Give Mademoiselle a hint that H. Wills should not be encouraged to put in injudicious appearances downstairs.

December 13*th.*—Ram resumes activities. Helen Wills still with us.

December 16*th.*—Very stormy weather, floods out and many trees prostrated at inconvenient angles. Call from Lady Boxe, who says that she is off to the South of France next week, as she Must have Sunshine. She asks Why I do not go there too, and likens me to piece of chewed string, which I feel to be entirely inappropriate and rather offensive figure of speech, though perhaps kindly meant.

Why not just pop into the train, enquires Lady B., pop across France, and pop out into Blue Sky, Blue Sea, and Summer Sun? Could make perfectly comprehensive reply to this, but do not do so, question of expense having evidently not crossed Lady B.'s horizon. (*Mem.*: Interesting subject for debate at Women's Institute, perhaps: That Imagination is incompatible with Inherited Wealth. On second thoughts, though, fear this has a socialistic trend.)

Reply to Lady B. with insincere professions of liking England very much even in the Winter. She begs me not to let myself become parochially-minded.

Departure of Lady B. with many final appeals to me to reconsider South of France. Make civil pretence, which deceives neither of us, of wavering, and promise to ring her up in the event of a change of mind.

(Query: Cannot many of our moral lapses from Truth be frequently charged upon the tactless persistence of others?)

December 17*th*, *London.*—Come up to dear Rose's flat for two days' Christmas shopping, after prolonged discussion with Robert, who maintains that All can equally well be done by Post.

Take early train so as to get in extra afternoon. Have with me Robert's old leather suit-case, own ditto in fibre, large quantity of chrysanthemums done up in brown paper for Rose, small packet of sandwiches, handbag, fur coat in case weather turns cold, book for journey, and illustrated paper kindly presented by Mademoiselle at the station. (Query: suggests itself: Could not some of these things have been dispensed with, and if so which?)

Bestow belongings in the rack, and open illustrated paper with sensation of leisured opulence, derived from unwonted absence of all domestic duties.

Unknown lady enters carriage at first stop, and takes seat opposite. She has expensive - looking luggage in moderate quantity, and small red morocco jewel-case, also bran-new copy, without library label, of *Life of Sir Edward Marshall-Hall.* Am reminded of Lady B. and have recrudescence of Inferiority Complex.

Remaining seats occupied by elderly

gentleman wearing spats, nondescript female in a Burberry, and young man strongly resembling an Arthur Watts drawing. He looks at a copy of *Punch*, and I spend much time in wondering if it contains an Arthur Watts drawing and if he is struck by resemblance, and if so what his reactions are, whether of pain or gratification.

Roused from these unprofitable, but sympathetic, considerations by agitation on the part of elderly gentleman, who says that, upon his soul, he is being dripped upon. Everybody looks at ceiling, and Burberry female makes a vague reference to unspecified "pipes" which she declares often "go like that". Someone else madly suggests turning off the heat. Elderly gentleman refuses all explanations and declares that *It comes from the rack*. We all look with horror at Rose's chrysanthemums, from which large drips of water descend regularly. Am overcome with shame, remove chrysanthemums, apologise to elderly gentleman, and sit down again opposite to superior unknown, who has remained glued to *Sir E. Marshall-Hall* throughout, and reminds me of Lady B. more than ever.

(*Mem.*: Speak to Mademoiselle about officiousness of thrusting flowers into water unasked, just before wrapping up.)

Immerse myself in illustrated weekly. Am informed by it that Lord Toto Finch (inset) is responsible for camera-study (herewith) of the Loveliest Legs in Los Angeles, belonging to well-known English Society girl, near relation (by the way) of famous racing peer, father of well-known Smart Set twins (portrait overleaf).

(Query: Is our popular Press going to the dogs?)

Turn attention to short story, but give it up on being directed, just as I become interested, to page *XLVIIb*, which I am quite unable to locate. Become involved instead with suggestions for Christmas Gifts. I want my gifts, the writer assures me, to be individual and yet appropriate—

beautiful, and yet enduring. Then why not Enamel dressing-table set, at £94 16s. 4d. or Set of crystal-ware, exact replica of early English cut-glass, at moderate price of £34 17s. 9d.?

Why not, indeed?

Am touched to discover further on, however, explicit reference to Giver with Restricted Means—though even here, am compelled to differ from author's definition of restricted means. Let originality of thought, she says, add character to trifling offering. Would not many of my friends welcome suggestion of a course of treatment—(six for 5 guineas)—at Madame Dolly Varden's Beauty Parlour in Piccadilly to be placed to my account?

Cannot visualise myself making this offer to our Vicar's wife, still less her reception of it, and decide to confine myself to one-and-sixpenny calendar with picture of sunset on Scaw Fell, as usual.

(Indulge, on the other hand, in a few moments' idle phantasy, in which I suggest to Lady B. that she should accept from me as a graceful and appropriate Christmas gift, a course of Reducing Exercises accompanied by Soothing and Wrinkle-eradicating Face Massage.)

This imaginative exercise brought to a conclusion by arrival.

Obliged to take taxi from station, mainly owing to chrysanthemums (which would not combine well with two suit-cases and fur coat on moving stairway, which I distrust and dislike anyhow, and am only too apt to make conspicuous failure of Stepping Off with Right Foot foremost)—but also partly owing to fashionable locality of Rose's flat, miles removed from any Underground.

Kindest welcome from dear Rose, who is most appreciative of chrysanthemums. Refrain from mentioning unfortunate incident with elderly gentleman in train.

December 19*th.*—Find Christmas shopping very exhausting. Am paralysed in the Army and Navy Stores on discovering that

List of Xmas Presents is lost, but eventually run it to earth in Children's Books Department. While there choose book for dear Robin, and wish for the hundredth time that Vicky had been less definite about wanting Toy Greenhouse and *nothing else*. This apparently unprocurable. (*Mem.*: Take early opportunity of looking up story of the Roc's Egg to tell Vicky.)

Rose says "Try Selfridge's." I protest, but eventually go there, find admirable—though expensive—Toy Greenhouse, and unpatriotically purchase it at once. Decide not to tell Robert this.

Choose appropriate offerings for Rose, Mademoiselle, William, and Angela—(who will be staying with us, so gifts must be above calendar-mark)—and lesser trifles for everyone else. Unable to decide between almost invisibly small diary, and really handsome card, for Cissie Crabbe, but eventually settle on diary, as it will fit into ordinary-sized envelope.

December 20th.—Rose takes me to see St. John Ervine's play, and am much amused. Overhear one lady in stalls ask another: Why don't *you* write a play, dear? Well, says the friend, it's so difficult, what with one thing and another, to find *time.* Am staggered. (Query: Could I write a play myself? Could we *all* write plays, if only we had the time? Reflect that St. J. E. lives in the same county as myself, but feel that this does not constitute sound excuse for writing to ask him how he finds the time to write plays.)

December 22nd.—Return home. One bulb in partial flower, but not satisfactory.

December 23rd.—Meet Robin at the Junction. He has lost his ticket, parcel of sandwiches, and handkerchief, but produces large wooden packing-case, into which little shelf has been wedged. Understand that this represents result of Carpentry Class—expensive "extra" at school—and is a Christmas present. Will no doubt appear on bill in due course.

Robin says essential to get gramophone record called "Is Izzy Azzy Wozz?" (*N.B.* Am often struck by disquieting thought that the dear children are entirely devoid of any artistic feeling whatever, in art, literature, or music. This conviction intensified after hearing "Is Izzy Azzy Wozz?" rendered fourteen times running on the gramophone, after I have succeeded in obtaining record.)

Much touched at enthusiastic greeting between Robin and Vicky. Mademoiselle says, "Ah, c'est gentil!" and produces a handkerchief, which I think exaggerated, especially as in half-an-hour's time she comes to me with complaint that R. and V. have gone up into the rafters and are shaking down plaster from nursery ceiling. Remonstrate with them from below. They sing "Is Izzy Azzy Wozz?" Am distressed at this, as providing fresh confirmation of painful conviction that neither has any ear for music, nor ever will have.

Arrival of William and Angela, at half-past three. Should like to hurry up tea, but feel that servants would be annoyed, so instead offer to show them their rooms, which they know perfectly well already. We exchange news about relations. Robin and Vicky appear, still singing "Is Izzy Azzy Wozz?" Angela says that they have grown. Can see by her expression that she thinks them odious, and very badly brought-up. She tells me about the children in the last house she stayed at. All appear to have been miracles of cleanliness, intelligence, and charm. A. also adds, most unnecessarily, that they are musical, and play the piano nicely.

(*Mem.*: A meal the most satisfactory way of entertaining any guest. Should much like to abridge the interval between tea and dinner—or else to introduce supplementary collation in between.)

At dinner we talk again about relations, and ask one another if anything is ever heard of poor Frederick, nowadays, and how Mollie's marriage is turning out, and whether Grandmama is thinking of going to the East Coast again this summer. Am annoyed because Robert and William sit on in the dining-room until nearly ten o'clock, which makes the servants late.

December 24th.—Take entire family to children's party at neighbouring Rectory. Robin says Damn three times in the Rector's hearing, an expression never used by him before or since, but apparently reserved for this unsuitable occasion. Party otherwise highly successful, except that I again meet recent arrival at the Grange, on whom I have not yet called. She is a Mrs. Somers, and is said to keep Bees. Find myself next to her at tea, but cannot think of anything to say about Bees, except Does she *like* them, which sounds like a bad riddle, so leave it unsaid and talk about Preparatory Schools instead. (Am interested to note that no two parents ever seem to have heard of one another's Preparatory Schools. Query: Can this indicate an undue number of these establishments throughout the country?)

After dinner, get presents ready for children's stockings. William unfortunately steps on small glass article of doll's furniture intended for Vicky, but handsomely offers a shilling in compensation, which I refuse. Much time taken up in discussing this. At eleven P.M. children still wide awake. Angela suggests Bridge and asks Who is that Mrs. Somers we met at the Rectory, who seems to be interested in Bees? (A. evidently more skilled than myself in social amenities, but do not make this comment aloud.)

Xmas Day. — Festive, but exhausting, Christmas. Robin and Vicky delighted with everything, and spend much of the day eating. Vicky presents her Aunt Angela with small square of canvas on which blue donkey is worked in cross-stitch. Do not know whether to apologise for this or not, but eventually decide better to say nothing, and hint to Mademoiselle that other design might have been preferable.

The children perhaps rather too much *en évidence*, as Angela, towards tea-time, begins to tell me that the little Maitlands have such a delightful nursery, and always spend entire day in it except when out for long walks with governess and dogs.

William asks if that Mrs. Somers is one of the *Dorsetshire* lot—a woman who knows about Bees.

Make a note that I really must call on Mrs. S. early next week. Read up something about Bees before going.

Turkey and plum-pudding cold in the evening, to give servants a rest. Angela looks at bulbs, and says What made me think they would be in flower for Christmas? Do not reply to this, but suggest early bed for us all.

December 27th.—Departure of William and Angela. Slight shock administered at eleventh hour by Angela, who asks if I realise that *she* was winner of first prize in last week's *Time and Tide* Competition, under the pseudonym of *Intelligensia*. Had naturally no idea of this, but congratulate her, without mentioning that I entered for same competition myself, without success.

(Query: Are Competition Editors always sound on questions of literary merit? Judgement possibly becomes warped through overwork.)

Another children's party this afternoon, too large and elaborate. Mothers stand about it in black hats and talk to one another about gardens, books, and difficulty of getting servants to stay in the country. Tea handed about the hall in a detached way, while children are herded into another room. Vicky and Robin behave well, and I compliment them on the way home, but am informed later by Mademoiselle that she has found large collection of chocolate biscuits in pocket of Vicky's party-frock.

(*Mem.*: Would it be advisable to point out

to Vicky that this constitutes failure in intelligence, as well as in manners, hygiene, and common honesty?)

January 1st, 1930.—We give a children's party ourselves. Very, very exhausting performance, greatly complicated by stormy weather, which keeps half the guests away, and causes grave fears as to arrival of the conjurer.

Decide to have children's tea in the dining-room, grown-ups in the study, and clear the drawing-room for games and conjurer. Minor articles of drawing-room furniture moved up to my bedroom, where I continually knock myself against them. Bulb-bowls greatly in everybody's way and are put on window-ledges in passage, at which Mademoiselle says: "Tiens! ça fait un drôle d'effet, ces malheureux petits brins de verdure!" Do not like this description at all.

The children from neighbouring Rectory arrive too early, and are shown into completely empty drawing-room. Entrance of Vicky, in new green party-frock, with four balloons, saves situation.

(Query: What is the reason that clerical households are always unpunctual, invariably arriving either first, or last, at any gathering to which bidden?)

Am struck at variety of behaviour amongst mothers, some so helpful in organising games and making suggestions, others merely sitting about. (*N.B.* For sake of honesty, should rather say *standing* about, as supply of chairs fails early.) Resolve always to send Robin and Vicky to parties without me, if possible, as children without parents infinitely preferable from point of view of hostess. Find it difficult to get "Oranges and Lemons" going, whilst at same time appearing to give intelligent attention to remarks from visiting mother concerning Exhibition of Italian Pictures at Burlington House. Find myself telling her how marvellous I think them, although in actual fact have not yet seen them at all. Realise that this mis-statement should be corrected at once, but omit to do so, and later find myself involved in entirely unintentional web of falsehood. Should like to work out how far morally to blame for this state of things, but have not time.

Tea goes off well. Mademoiselle presides in dining-room, I in study. Robert and solitary elderly father—(looks more like a grandfather)—stand in doorway and talk about big-game shooting and the last General Election, in intervals of handing tea.

Conjurer arrives late, but is a success with children. Ends up with presents from a bran-tub, in which more bran is spilt on carpet, children's clothes, and house generally, than could ever have been got into tub originally. Think this odd, but have noticed similar phenomenon before.

Guests depart between seven and half-past, and Helen Wills and the dog are let out by Robin, having been shut up on account of crackers, which they dislike.

Robert and I spend evening helping servants to restore order, and trying to

remember where ash-trays, clock, orna-
ments, and ink were put for safety.

January 3rd.—Hounds meet in the village. Robert agrees to take Vicky on the
pony. Robin, Mademoiselle, and I walk to
the Post Office to see the start, and Robin
talks about Oliver Twist, making no reference whatever to hunt from start to finish,
and viewing horses, hounds, and huntsmen
with equal detachment. Am impressed at
his non-suggestibility, but feel that some
deep Freudian significance may lie behind
it all. Feel also that Robert would take very
different view of it.

Meet quantities of hunting neighbours,
who say to Robin, "Aren't you riding *too?*"
which strikes one as lacking in intelligence,
and ask me if we have lost many trees lately,
but do not wait for answer, as what they
really want to talk about is the number of
trees they have lost themselves.

Mademoiselle looks at hounds and says,
"Ah, ces bons chiens!" also admires horses,

"quelles bêtes superbes"—but prudently keeps well away from all, in which I follow her example.

Vicky looks nice on pony, and I receive compliments about her, which I accept in an off-hand manner, tinged with incredulity, in order to show that I am a modern mother and should scorn to be foolish about my children.

Hunt moves off, Mademoiselle remarking, "Voilà bien le sport anglais!" Robin says: "Now can we go home?" and eats milk-chocolate. We return to the house and I write order to the Stores, post-card to the butcher, two letters about Women's Institutes, one about Girl Guides, note to the dentist asking for appointment next week, and make memorandum in engagement-book that I *must* call on Mrs. Somers at the Grange.

Am horrified and incredulous at discovery that these occupations have filled the entire morning.

Robert and Vicky return late, Vicky

plastered with mud from head to foot but unharmed. Mademoiselle removes her, and says no more about *le sport anglais*.

January 4th.—A beautiful day, very mild, makes me feel that with any reasonable luck Mrs. Somers will be out, and I therefore call at the Grange. She is, on the contrary, in. Find her in the drawing-room, wearing printed velvet frock that I immediately think would look nice on *me*. No sign anywhere of Bees, but am getting ready to enquire about them intelligently when Mrs. Somers suddenly says that her Mother is here, and knows my old school-friend Cissie Crabbe, who says that I am so *amusing*. The Mother comes in—very elegant Marcel wave — (cannot imagine where she got it, unless she has this moment come from London)—and general air of knowing how to dress in the country. She is introduced to me—name sounds exactly like Eggchalk but do not think this possible—and says she knows my old school-friend Miss Crabbe, at Norwich, and has heard all about how very, very amusing I am. Become completely paralysed and can think of nothing whatever to say except that it has been very stormy lately. Leave as soon as possible.

January 5th.—Rose, in the kindest way, offers to take me as her guest to special dinner of famous Literary Club if I will come up to London for the night. Celebrated editor of literary weekly paper in the chair, spectacularly successful author of famous play as guest of honour. Principal authors, poets, and artists from— says Rose—all over the world, expected to be present.

Spend much of the evening talking to Robert about this. Put it to him: (*a*) That no expense is involved beyond 3rd class return ticket to London; (*b*) that in another twelve years Vicky will be coming out, and it is therefore incumbent on me to Keep in Touch with People; (*c*) that this is an opportunity that will never occur again; (*d*) that it isn't as if I were asking him to come too. Robert says nothing to (*a*) or (*b*) and only "I should hope not" to (*c*), but appears slightly moved by (*d*). Finally says he supposes I must do as I like, and very likely I shall meet some old friends of my Bohemian days when living with Rose in Hampstead.

Am touched by this, and experience passing wonder if Robert can be feeling slightly jealous. This fugitive idea dispelled by his immediately beginning to speak about failure of hot water this morning.

January 7th.—Rose takes me to Literary Club dinner. I wear my Blue. Am much struck by various young men who have defiantly put on flannel shirts and no ties, and brushed their hair up on end. They are mostly accompanied by red-headed young women who wear printed crêpe frocks and beads. Otherwise, everyone in evening dress. Am introduced to distin-

guished Editor, who turns out to be female
and delightful. Should like to ask her once
and for all why prizes in her paper's weekly
competition are so often divided, but feel
this would be unsuitable and put Rose to
shame.

Am placed at dinner next to celebrated
best-seller, who tells me in the kindest way
how to evade paying super-tax. Am easily
able to conceal from him the fact that I am
not at present in a position to require this
information. Very distinguished artist sits
opposite, and becomes more and more
convivial as evening advances. This encourages me to remind him that we have
met before—which we have, in old Hampstead days. He declares enthusiastically
that he remembers me perfectly—which
we both know to be entirely untrue—and
adds wildly that he has followed my work
ever since. Feel it better to let this pass un-
challenged. Later on, distinguished artist
is found to have come out without any
money, and all in his immediate neighbour-

hood are required to lend him amount demanded by head-waiter.

Feel distinctly thankful that Robert is not with me, and am moreover morally certain that distinguished artist will remember nothing whatever in the morning, and will therefore be unable to refund my three-and-sixpence.

Rose handsomely pays for my dinner as well as her own.

(This suggests *Mem*.: That English cooking, never unduly attractive, becomes positively nauseating on any public occasion, such as a banquet. Am seriously distressed at probable reactions of foreign visitors to this evening's fish, let alone other items.)

Young gentleman is introduced to me by Rose—(she saying in rapid murmur that he is part-author of a one-act play that has been acted three times by a Repertory company in Jugo-Slavia.) It turns out later that he has met Lady Boxe, who struck him, he adds immediately, as a poisonous woman. We then get on well together. (Query: Is not a common hate one of the strongest links in human nature? Answer, most regrettably, in the affirmative.)

Very, very distinguished Novelist approaches me (having evidently mistaken me for someone else), and talks amiably. She says that she can only write between twelve at night and four in the morning, and not always then. When she cannot write, she plays the organ. Should much like to ask whether she is married—but get no opportunity of asking that or anything else. She tells me about her sales. She tells me about her last book. She tells me about her new one. She says that there are many people here to whom she *must* speak, and pursues well-known Poet—who does not, however, allow her to catch up with him. Can understand this.

Speeches are made. Am struck, as so often, by the eloquence and profundity of other people, and reflect how sorry I should be to have to make a speech myself, although so often kept awake at night com-

"VERY, VERY DISTINGUISHED NOVELIST."

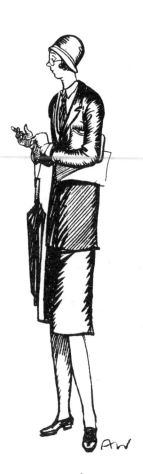

THE VICAR'S WIFE.

posing wholly admirable addresses to the servants, Lady B., Mademoiselle, and others—
which, however, never get delivered.

Move about after dinner, and meet acquaintance whose name I have forgotten,
but connect with literature. I ask if he has
published anything lately. He says that his
work is not, and never can be, for publica-
tion. Thought passes through my mind to
the effect that this attitude might with advantage be adopted by many others. Do
not say so, however, and we talk instead
about Rebecca West, the progress of avia-
tion, and the case for and against stag-
hunting.

Rose, who has been discussing psychiatry
as practised in the U.S.A. with Danish
journalist, says Am I ready to go? Distinguished artist who sat opposite me at dinner
offers to drive us both home, but his friends
intervene. Moreover, acquaintance whose
name I have forgotten takes me aside, and
assures me that D.A. is quite unfit to take
anybody home, and will himself require

an escort. Rose and I depart by nearest Tube, as being wiser, if less exalted, procedure.

Sit up till one o'clock discussing our fellow-creatures, with special reference to those seen and heard this evening. Rose says I ought to come to London more often, and suggests that outlook requires broadening.

January 9th.—Came home yesterday. Robin and Mademoiselle no longer on speaking terms, owing to involved affair centering round a broken window-pane. Vicky, startlingly, tells me in private that she has learnt a new Bad Word, but does not mean to use it. Not now, anyway, she disquietingly adds.

Cook says she hopes I enjoyed my holiday, and it is very quiet in the country. I leave the kitchen before she has time to say more, but am only too well aware that this is not the last of it.

Write grateful letter to Rose, at the same

time explaining difficulty of broadening my outlook by further time spent away from home, just at present.

January 14*th*.—I have occasion to observe, not for the first time, how extraordinarily plain a cold can make one look, affecting hair, complexion, and features generally, besides nose and upper lip. Cook assures me that colds always run through the house and that she herself has been suffering from sore throat for weeks, but is never one to make a fuss. (Query: Is this meant to imply that similar fortitude should be, but is not, displayed by me?) Mademoiselle says she *hopes* children will not catch my cold, but that both sneezed this morning. I run short of handkerchiefs.

January 16*th*.—We all run short of handkerchiefs.

January 17*th*.—Mademoiselle suggests butter-muslin. There is none in the house.

I say that I will go out and buy some. Mademoiselle says, "No, the fresh air gives pneumonia." Feel that I ought to combat this un-British attitude, but lack energy, especially when she adds that she will go herself—"Madame, j'y cours." She puts on black kid gloves, buttoned boots with pointed tips and high heels, hat with little feather in it, black jacket and several silk neckties, and goes, leaving me to amuse Robin and Vicky, both in bed. Twenty minutes after she has started, I remember it is early-closing day.

Go up to night-nursery and offer to read Lamb's *Tales from Shakespeare*. Vicky says she prefers *Pip, Squeak, and Wilfred*. Robin says that he would like *Gulliver's Travels*. Compromise on *Grimm's Fairy Tales*, although slightly uneasy as to their being in accordance with best modern ideals. Both children take immense interest in story of highly undesirable person who wins fortune, fame, and beautiful Princess by means of lies, violence, and treachery. Feel sure that this must have disastrous effect on both in years to come.

Our Vicar's wife calls before Mademoiselle returns. Go down to her, sneezing, and suggest that she had better not stay. She says, much better not, and she won't keep me a minute. Tells me long story about the Vicar having a stye on one eye. I retaliate with Cook's sore throat. This leads to draughts, the heating apparatus in church, and news of Lady Boxe in South of France. The Vicar's wife has had a picture postcard from her (which she produces from bag), with small cross marking bedroom window of hotel. She says, It's rather interesting, isn't it? to which I reply Yes, it is, very, which is not in the least true. (*N.B.* Truth-telling in everyday life extraordinarily difficult. Is this personal, and highly deplorable, idiosyncrasy, or do others suffer in the same way? Have momentary impulse to put this to our Vicar's wife, but decide better not.)

How, she says, are the dear children, and

how is my husband? I reply suitably, and
she tells me about cinnamon, Vapex, gar-
gling with glycerine of thymol, black-
currant tea, onion broth, friar's balsam,
linseed poultices, and thermogene wool.
I sneeze and say Thank you—thank you
very much, a good many times. She goes,
but turns back at the door to tell me about
wool next the skin, nasal douching, and
hot milk last thing at night. I say Thank
you, again.

On returning to night-nursery, find that
Robin has unscrewed top of hot-water
bottle in Vicky's bed, which apparently
contained several hundred gallons of tepid
water, now distributed through and through
pillows, pyjamas, sheets, blankets, and mat-
tresses of both. I ring for Ethel, who helps
me to reorganise entire situation and says
It's like a hospital, isn't it, trays up and down
stairs all day long, and all this extra work.

January 20th.—Take Robin, now completely restored, back to school. I ask the

Headmaster what he thinks of his progress. The Headmaster answers that the New Buildings will be finished before Easter, and that their numbers are increasing so rapidly that he will probably add on a New Wing next term, and perhaps I saw a letter of his in the *Times* replying to Dr. Cyril Norwood? Make mental note to the effect that Headmasters are a race apart, and that if parents would remember this, much time could be saved.

Robin and I say good-bye with hideous brightness, and I cry all the way back to the station.

January 22nd.—Robert startles me at breakfast by asking if my cold—which he has hitherto ignored—is better. I reply that it has gone. Then why, he asks, do I look like that? Refrain from asking like what, as I know only too well. Feel that life is wholly unendurable, and decide madly to get a new hat.

Customary painful situation between

Bank and myself necessitates expedient, also customary, of pawning great-aunt's diamond ring, which I do, under usual conditions, and am greeted as old friend by Plymouth pawnbroker, who says facetiously, And what name will it be *this* time?

Visit four linen-drapers and try on several dozen hats. Look worse and worse in each one, as hair gets wilder and wilder, and expression paler and more harassed. Decide to get myself shampooed and waved before doing any more, in hopes of improving the position.

Hairdresser's assistant says, It's a pity my hair is losing all its colour, and have I ever thought of having it touched up? After long discussion, I do have it touched up, and emerge with mahogany-coloured head. Hairdresser's assistant says this will wear off "in a few days". I am very angry, but all to no purpose. Return home in old hat, showing as little hair as possible, and keep it on till dressing time—but cannot hope to conceal my shame at dinner.

January 23rd.—Mary Kellway telegraphs she is motoring past here this morning, can I give her lunch? Telegraph Yes, delighted, and rush to kitchen. Cook unhelpful and suggests cold beef and beetroot. I say Yes, excellent, unless perhaps roast chicken and bread sauce even better? Cook talks about the oven. Compromise in the end on cutlets and mashed potatoes, as, very luckily, this is the day butcher calls.

Always delighted to see dear Mary—so clever and amusing, and able to write stories, which actually get published and paid for—but very uneasy about colour of my hair, which is not wearing off in the least. Think seriously of keeping a hat on all through lunch, but this, on the whole, would look even more unnatural. Besides, could not hope that it would pass without observation from Vicky, let alone Robert.

Later.—Worst fears realised, as to hair. Dear Mary, always so observant, gazes at it in nerve-shattering silence but says nothing, till I am driven to make half-hearted explanation. Her only comment is that she cannot imagine why anybody should deliberately make themselves look ten years older than they need. Feel that, if she wishes to discourage further experiments on my part, this observation could scarcely be improved upon. Change the subject, and talk about the children. Mary most sympathetic, and goes so far as to say that *my* children have brains, which encourages me to tell anecdotes about them until I see Robert looking at me, just as I get to Robin's precocious taste for really good literature. By curious coincidence second post brings letter from Robin, saying that he wishes to collect cigarette-cards and will I send him all the types of National Beauty, Curious Beaks, and Famous Footballers, that I can find. Make no comment on this singular request aloud.

Mary stays to tea and we talk about H. G. Wells, Women's Institutes, infectious illness, and *Journey's End*. Mary says she cannot go and see this latter because she always cries at the theatre. I say, Then once more will make no difference. Discussion becomes involved, and we drop it. Vicky comes in and immediately offers to recite. Can see that Mary (who has three children of her own) does not in the least want to hear her, but she feigns enthusiasm politely. Vicky recites: "Maître Corbeau sur un arbre perché"—(*N.B.* Suggest to Mademoiselle that Vicky's repertory should be enlarged. Feel sure that I have heard Maître Corbeau, alternately with La Cigale et la Fourmi, some eight hundred times within the last six months.)

After Mary has gone, Robert looks at me and suddenly remarks: "Now *that's* what I call an attractive woman." Am gratified at his appreciation of talented friend, but should like to be a little clearer regarding exact significance of emphasis on the word *that*. Robert, however, says no more, and opportunity is lost as Ethel comes in to say Cook is sorry she's run right out of milk, but if I will come to the store-cupboard she thinks there's a tin of Ideal, and she'll make do with that.

January 25th.—Attend a Committee Meeting in the village to discuss how to raise funds for Village Hall. Am asked to take the chair. Begin by saying that I know how much we all have this excellent object at heart, and that I feel sure there will be no lack of suggestions as to best method of obtaining requisite sum of money. Pause for suggestions, which is met with death-like silence. I say, There are so many ways to choose from—implication being that I attribute silence to plethora of ideas, rather than to absence of them. (*Note*: Curious and rather depressing, to see how frequently the pursuit of Good Works leads to apparently unavoidable duplicity.) Silence continues, and I say Well, twice, and Come, come, once. (Sudden impulse to exclaim, "I lift up my finger and I say Tweet, Tweet," is fortunately overcome.) At last extract a suggestion of a concert from Mrs. L. (whose son plays the violin) and a whist-drive from Miss P. (who won Ladies' First Prize at the last one). Florrie P. suggests a dance and is at once reminded that it will be Lent. She says that Lent isn't what it was. Her mother says the Vicar is one that holds with Lent, and always has been. Someone else says That reminds her, has anyone heard that old Mr. Small passed away last night? We all agree that eighty-six is a great age. Mrs. L. says that on her mother's side of the family, there is an aunt of ninety-eight. Still with us, she adds. The aunt's husband, on the other hand, was gathered just before his sixtieth birthday. Everyone says, You can't ever *tell*, not really. There is a suitable pause before we go back to Lent and the Vicar. General opinion that a concert isn't like a dance, and needn't—says Mrs. L.—interfere.

On this understanding, we proceed. Various familiar items—piano solo, recitation, duet, and violin solo from Master L.— are all agreed upon. Someone says that Mrs. F. and Miss H. might do a dialogue, and has to be reminded that they are no longer on speaking terms, owing to strange behaviour of Miss H. about her bantams. Ah, says Mrs. S., it wasn't only *bantams* was at the bottom of it, there's two sides to every question. (There are at least twenty to this one, by the time we've done with it.)

Sudden appearance of our Vicar's wife, who says apologetically that she made a mistake in the time. I beg her to take the chair. She refuses. I insist. She says No, no, positively not, and takes it.

We begin all over again, but general attitude towards Lent much less elastic.

Meeting ends at about five o'clock. Our Vicar's wife walks home with me, and tells me that I look tired. I ask her to come in and have tea. No, she says, no, it's too kind of me, but she must go on to the far end of the parish. She remains standing at the gate telling me about old Small—eighty-six a great age—till quarter-to-six, when she departs, saying that she cannot *think* why I am looking so tired.

February 11*th*.—Robin writes again about cigarette-cards. I send him all those I have collected, and Vicky produces two which she has obtained from the garden-boy. Find that this quest grows upon one, and am apt now, when in Plymouth or any other town, to scan gutters, pavements, and tram-floors in search of Curious Beaks, Famous Football Players, and the like. Have even gone so far as to implore perfect stranger, sitting opposite me in train, *not* to throw cigarette-card out of the window, but give it to me instead. Perfect stranger does so with an air of courteous astonishment, and as he asks for no explanation, am obliged to leave him under the impression that I have merely been trying to force him into conversation with me.

(*Note*: Could not short article, suitable for *Time and Tide*, be worked up on some such lines as: Lengths to which Mother-love may legitimately go? On second thoughts abandon the idea, as being faintly reminiscent of *démodé* enquiry: Do Shrimps make Good Mothers?)

Hear that Lady Boxe has returned from South of France and is entertaining house-party. She sends telephone message by the butler, asking me to tea to-morrow. I accept. (Why?)

February 12th.—Insufferable behaviour of Lady B. Find large party, all of whom are directed at front door to go to the Hard Courts, where, under inadequate shelter, in Arctic temperature, all are compelled to watch young men in white flannels keeping themselves warm by banging a little ball against a wall. Lady B. wears an emerald-green leather coat with fur collar and cuffs. I, having walked down, have on ordinary coat and skirt, and freeze rapidly. Find myself next unknown lady who talks wistfully about the tropics. Can well understand this. On other side elderly gentleman, who says conversationally that this Naval Disarmament is All his Eye. This contribution made to contemporary thought, he says no more. Past five o'clock before we are allowed to

LADY B.

"CAN HEAR ROBERT'S NEIGHBOUR . . . TELLING HIM ABOUT HER CHILBLAINS."

go in to tea, by which time am only too well aware that my face is blue and my hands purple. Lady B. asks me at tea how the children are, and adds, to the table at large, that I am "A Perfect Mother". Am naturally avoided, conversationally, after this, by everybody at the tea-table. Later on, Lady B. tells us about South of France. She quotes repartees made by herself in French, and then translates them.

(Unavoidable Query presents itself here: Would a verdict of Justifiable Homicide delivered against their mother affect future careers of children unfavourably?)

Discuss foreign travel with unknown, but charming, lady in black. We are delighted with one another—or so I confidently imagine—and she begs me to go and see her if I am ever in her neighbourhood. I say that I will—but am well aware that courage will fail me when it comes to the point. Pleasant sense of mutual sympathy suddenly and painfully shattered by my admitting—in reply to direct enquiry—that I am *not* a gardener—which the lady in black *is*, to an extent that apparently amounts to monomania. She remains charming, but quite ceases to be delighted with me, and I feel discouraged.

(*N.B. Must* try to remember that Social Success is seldom the portion of those who habitually live in the provinces. No doubt they serve some other purpose in the vast field of Creation—but have not yet discovered what.)

Lady B. asks if I have seen the new play at the Royalty. I say No. She says Have I been to the Italian Art Exhibition? I have not. She enquires what I think of *Her Privates We*—which I haven't yet read—and I at once give her a long and spirited account of my reactions to it. Feel after this that I had better go, before I am driven to further excesses.

Shall she, says Lady B., ring for my car? Refrain from replying that no amount of ringing will bring my car to the door all by itself, and say instead that I walked. Lady

B. exclaims that this is Impossible, and that I am Too Marvellous, Altogether. Take my leave before she can add that I am such a Perfect Countrywoman, which I feel is coming next.

Get home—still chilled to the bone owing to enforced detention at Hard Court—and tell Robert what I think of Lady B. He makes no answer, but I feel he agrees.

Mademoiselle says: "Tiens! Madame a mauvaise mine. On dirait un cadavre. . . ."

Feel that this is kindly meant, but do not care about the picture that it conjures up.

Say good-night to Vicky, looking angelic in bed, and ask what she is thinking about, lying there. She disconcertingly replies with briskness: "Oh, Kangaroos and things."

(*Note*: The workings of the infant mind very, very difficult to follow, sometimes. Mothers by no means infallible.)

February 14*th*.—Have won first prize in *Time and Tide* competition, but again divided. Am very angry indeed, and write excellent letter to the Editor under false name, protesting against this iniquitous custom. After it has gone, become seriously uneasy under the fear that the use of a false name is illegal. Look through *Whitaker*, but can find nothing but Stamp Duties and Concealment of Illegitimate Births, so abandon it in disgust.

Write to Angela—under my own name— to enquire kindly if *she* went in for the competition. Hope she did, and that she will have the decency to say so.

February 16*th*.—Informed by Ethel, as she calls me in the morning, that Helen Wills has had six kittens, of which five survive.

Cannot imagine how I shall break this news to Robert. Reflect—not for the first time—that the workings of Nature are most singular.

Angela writes that she *didn't* go in for competition, thinking the subject puerile, but that she solved "Merope's" Cross-word puzzle in fifteen minutes.

(*N.B.* This last statement almost certainly inaccurate.)

February 21*st.*—Remove bulb-bowls, with what is left of bulbs, to greenhouse. Tell Robert that I hope to do better another year. He replies, Another year, better not waste my money. This reply depresses me, moreover weather continues Arctic, and have by no means recovered from effects of Lady B.'s so-called hospitality.

Vicky and Mademoiselle spend much time in boot-cupboard, where Helen Wills is established with five kittens. Robert still unaware of what has happened, but cannot hope this ignorance will continue. Must, however, choose suitable moment for revelation—which is unlikely to occur to-day owing to bath-water having been cold again this morning.

Lady B. calls in the afternoon—not, as might have been expected, to see if I am in bed with pneumonia, but to ask if I will help at a Bazaar early in May. Further enquiry reveals that it is in aid of the Party Funds. I say What Party? (Am well aware of Lady B.'s political views, but resent having it taken for granted that mine are the same—which they are not.)

Lady B. says she is Surprised. Later on she says Look at the Russians, and even, Look at the Pope. I find myself telling her to Look at Unemployment—none of which gets us any further. Am relieved when tea comes in, and still more so when Lady B. says she really mustn't wait, as she has to call on such a number of Tenants. She asks after Robert, and I think seriously of replying that he is out receiving the Oath of Allegiance from all the vassals on the estate, but decide that this would be undignified.

Escort Lady B. to the hall-door. She tells me that the oak dresser would look better on the other side of the hall, and that it is a mistake to put mahogany and walnut in the same room. Her last word is that she will Write, about the bazaar. Relieve my feelings by waving small red flag belonging to

Vicky, which is lying on the hall-stand, and saying *A la lanterne!* as chauffeur drives off. Rather unfortunately, Ethel chooses this moment to walk through the hall. She says nothing, but looks astonished.

February 22nd.—Gloom prevails, owing to Helen Wills having elected, with incredible idiocy, to introduce progeny, one by one, to Robert's notice at late hour last night, when he was making final round of the house.

Send Mademoiselle and Vicky on errand to the village whilst massacre of the innocents takes place in pail of water in backyard. Small ginger is allowed to survive. Spend much time in thinking out plausible story to account to Vicky for disappearance of all the rest. Mademoiselle, when informed privately of what has happened, tells me to leave Vicky to her—which I gladly agree to do—and adds that "les hommes manquent de coeur". Feel that this is leading us in the direction of a story which I have heard before, and do not wish to hear again, regarding *un mariage échoué* arranged years ago for Mademoiselle by her parents, in which negotiations broke down owing to mercenary attitude of *le futur*. Break in with hasty enquiry regarding water-tightness or otherwise of Vicky's boots.

(Query: Does incessant pressure of domestic cares vitiate capacity for human sympathy? Fear that it does, but find myself unable to attempt reformation in this direction at present.)

Receive long, and in parts illegible, letter from Cissie Crabbe, bearing on the back of the envelope extraordinary enquiry: Do you know of a really *good* hotel Manageress? Combat strong inclination to reply on a postcard: No, but can recommend thoroughly reliable Dentist. Dear Cissie, one remembers from old school-days, has very little sense of humour.

February 24th.—Robert and I lunch with our Member and his wife. I sit next elderly gentleman who talks about stag-hunting and tells me that there is Nothing Cruel about it. The Stag *likes* it, and it is an honest, healthy, thoroughly *English* form of sport. I say Yes, as anything else would be waste of breath, and turn to Damage done by recent storms, New arrivals in the neighbourhood, and Golf-links at Budleigh Salterton. Find that we get back to stag-hunting again in next to no time, and remain there for the rest of lunch.

Can hear Robert's neighbour, sitting opposite in cochineal three-piece suit, telling him about her Chilblains. Robert civil, but does not appear unduly concerned. (Perhaps three-piece cochineal thinks that he is one of those people who feel more than they can express?) She goes on to past appendicitis, present sciatica, and threat of colitis in the near future. Robert still unmoved.

Ladies retire to the drawing-room and gather round quite inadequate fire. Coffee.

I perform my usual sleight-of-hand, transferring large piece of candy-sugar from saucer to handbag, for Vicky's benefit. (Query: Why do people living in same neighbourhood as myself obtain without difficulty minor luxuries that I am totally unable to procure? Reply to this, if pursued to logical conclusion, appears to point to inadequate housekeeping on my part.)

Entrance of males. I hear my neighbour at lunch beginning all over again about stag-hunting, this time addressed to his hostess, who is well-known supporter of the R.S.P.C.A.

Our Member talks to me about Football. I say that I think well of the French, and that Béhotéguy plays a good game. (*N.B.* This solitary piece of knowledge always coming in useful, but *must* try and find out name of at least one British player, so as to vary it.)

As we take our leave with customary graceful speeches, clasp of handbag unfortunately gives way, and piece of candy-sugar falls, with incredible noise and violence, on to the parquet, and is pursued with officious zeal and determination by all present except myself.

Very, very difficult moment. . . .

Robert, on the whole, takes this well, merely enquiring on the way home if I suppose that we shall ever be asked inside the house again.

February 28*th*.—Notice, and am gratified by, appearance of large clump of crocuses near the front gate. Should like to make whimsical and charming reference to these, and try to fancy myself as "Elizabeth of the German Garden", but am interrupted by Cook, saying that the Fish is here, but he's only brought cod and haddock, and the haddock doesn't smell any too fresh, so what about cod?

Have often noticed that Life is like that.

March 1*st*.—The Kellways lunch with us, before going on all together to wedding of Rosemary H., daughter of mutual friend and neighbour. Fire refuses to burn up, and am still struggling with it when they arrive, with small boy, Vicky's contemporary—all three frozen with cold. I say, Do come and get warm! and they accept this, alas meaningless, offer with enthusiasm. Vicky rushes in, and am struck, as usual, by the complete and utter straightness of her hair in comparison with that of practically every other child in the world. (Little Kellway has natural wave.)

Chickens over-done, and potatoes underdone. Meringues quite a success, especially with the children, though leading to brisk *sotto-voce* encounter between Vicky and Mademoiselle on question of second helping. This ends by an appeal from Mademoiselle for "un bon mouvement" on Vicky's part—which she facilitates by summarily removing her plate, spoon, and fork. Everybody ignores this drama, with the exception of the infant Kellway, who looks amused, and unblenchingly attacks a second meringue.

Start directly after lunch, Robert and Mary's husband appearing in a highly unnatural state of shiny smartness with a top-hat apiece. Effect of this splendour greatly mitigated, when they don the top-hats, by screams of unaffected amusement from both children. We drive off, leaving them leaning against Mademoiselle, apparently helpless with mirth.

(Query: Is not the inferiority complex, about which so much is written and spoken, nowadays shifting from the child to the parent?)

Mary wears blue with admirable diamond ornament, and looks nice. I wear red, and think regretfully of great-aunt's diamond ring, still reposing in back street of Plymouth, under care of old friend the pawnbroker. (*Note*: Financial situation very low indeed, and must positively take steps to send assortment of old clothes to second-hand dealer for disposal. Am struck by false air of opulence with which I don fur coat, white gloves, and new shoes—one very painful—and get into the car. Irony of life thus exemplified.)

Charming wedding, Rosemary H. looks lovely, bridesmaids highly picturesque. One of them has bright red hair, and am completely paralysed by devastating enquiry from Mary's husband, who hisses at me through his teeth: *Is that the colour yours was when you dyed it?*

Crowds of people at the reception. Know most of them, but am startled by strange lady in pink, wearing eye-glasses, who says that I don't remember her—which is only too true—but that she has played tennis at my house. How, she says, are those sweet twins? Find myself telling her that they are very well indeed, before I know where I am. Can only trust never to set eyes on her again.

Exchange talk with Mrs. Somers, recent arrival to the neighbourhood, who apologises profusely for never having returned my call. Am in doubt whether to say that I haven't noticed the omission, or that I hope she will repair it as quickly as possible. Either sounds uncivil.

Speak to old Lady Dufford, who reminds me that the last time we met was at the Jones wedding. *That*, she says, came to grief within a year. She also asks if I have heard about the Greens, who have separated, and poor Winifred R., who has had to go back to her parents because He drinks. Am not surprised when she concludes with observation that it is rather *heartrending* to see the two young things setting out together.

Large car belonging to bridegroom draws up at hall-door, and old Lady D. further wags her head at me and says Ah, in *our* day it would have been a carriage and pair —to which I offer no assent, thinking it very unnecessary reminder of the flight of Time—and in any event, am Lady D.'s junior by a good many years.

Melancholy engendered by the whole of this conversation is lightened by glass of champagne. I ask Robert, sentimentally, if this makes him think of *our* wedding. He looks surprised and says No, not particularly, why should it? As I cannot at the moment think of any particular reply to this, the question drops.

Departure of the bridal couple is followed by general exodus, and we take the Kellways home to tea.

Remove shoes with great thankfulness.

March 3rd.—Vicky, after Halma, enquires abruptly whether, if she died, I should cry? I reply in the affirmative. But, she says, should I cry really *hard*. Should I roar and scream? Decline to commit myself to any such extravagant demonstrations, at which Vicky displays a tendency to hurt astonishment. I speak to Mademoiselle and say that I hope she will discourage anything in Vicky that seems to verge upon the morbid. Mademoiselle requires a translation of the last word, and, after some consideration, I suggest *dénaturé*, at which she screams dramatically and crosses herself, and assures

VICKY.

MRS. BLENKINSOP.

me that if I knew what I was saying, I should "en reculer d'effroi".

We decide to abandon the subject.

Our Vicar's wife calls for me at seven o'clock, and we go to a neighbouring Women's Institute at which I have, rather rashly, promised to speak. On the way there, our Vicar's wife tells me that the secretary of the Institute is liable to have a heart attack at any minute and must on no account exert herself, or be allowed to get over-excited. Even a violent fit of laughing, she adds impressively, might carry her off in a moment.

Hastily revise my speech, and remove from it two funny stories. After this it is a shock to find that the programme for the evening includes dancing and a game of General Post. I ask our Vicar's wife what would happen if the secretary *did* get a heart attack, and she replies mysteriously, Oh, she always carries Drops in her handbag. The thing to do is to keep an eye on her handbag. This I do nervously throughout the evening, but fortunately no crisis supervenes.

I speak, am thanked, and asked if I will judge a Darning Competition. This I do, in spite of inward misgivings that few people are less qualified to give any opinion about darning than I am. I am thanked again and given tea and a doughnut. We all play General Post and get very heated. Signal success of the evening when two stout and elderly members collide in the middle of the room, and both fall heavily to the floor together. This, if anything, will surely bring on a heart attack, and am prepared to make a rush at the handbag, but nothing happens. We all sing the National Anthem, and our Vicar's wife says she does hope the lights of her two-seater are in order, and drives me home. We are relieved, and surprised, to find that the lights, all except the rear one, *are* in order, although rather faint.

I beg our Vicar's wife to come in; she says, No, No, it is far too late, really, and comes. Robert and Helen Wills both asleep in the drawing-room. Our Vicar's wife says she must not stay a moment, and we talk about Countrywomen, Stanley Baldwin, Hotels at Madeira (where none of us have ever been), and other unrelated topics. Ethel brings in cocoa, but can tell from the way she puts down the tray that she thinks it an unreasonable requirement, and will quite likely give notice to-morrow.

At eleven our Vicar's wife says that she *does* hope the lights of the two-seater are still in order, and gets as far as the hall-door. There we talk about forthcoming village concert, parrot-disease, and the Bishop of the diocese.

Her car refuses to start, and Robert and I push it down the drive. After a good deal of jerking and grinding, engine starts, the hand of our Vicar's wife waves at us through the hole in the talc, and car disappears down the lane.

Robert inhospitably says, let us put out the lights and fasten up the hall-door and go up to bed immediately, in case she comes back for anything. We do so, only delayed by Helen Wills, whom Robert tries vainly to expel into the night. She retires under the piano, behind the bookcase, and finally disappears altogether.

March 4th.—Ethel, as I anticipated, gives notice. Cook says this is so unsettling, she thinks she had better go too. Despair invades me. Write five letters to Registry Offices.

March 7th.—No hope.

March 8th.—Cook relents, so far as to say that she will stay until I am suited. Feel inclined to answer that, in that case, she had better make up her mind to a lifetime spent together—but naturally refrain. Spend exhausting day in Plymouth chasing mythical house-parlourmaids. Meet Lady B., who says the servant difficulty, in reality, is non-existent. She has NO trouble. It is a question of knowing how to treat them. Firmness, she says, but at the same time one must be human. Am I human? she asks. Do I understand that they want occasional diversion, just as I do myself? I lose my head and reply No, that it is my custom to keep my servants chained up in the cellar when their work is done. This flight of satire rather spoilt by Lady B. laughing heartily, and saying that I am always so amusing. Well, she adds, we shall no doubt see one another at lunch-time at the Duke of Cornwall Hotel, where alone it is possible to get a decent meal. I reply with ready cordiality that no doubt we shall, and go and partake of my usual lunch of baked beans and a glass of water in small and obscure café.

Unavoidable Query, of painfully searching character, here presents itself: If Lady B. had invited me as her guest to lunch at the D. of C. Hotel, should I have accepted? Am conscious of being heartily tired of baked beans and water, which in any case do not really serve to support one through long day of shopping and servant-hunting. Moreover, am always ready to See Life, in hotels or anywhere else. On the other hand, am aware that self-respect would suffer severely through accepting five-shillings-worth of luncheon from Lady B. Ponder this problem of psychology in train on the way home, but reach no definite conclusion.

Day a complete failure as regards house-parlourmaid, but expedition not wasted, having found two cigarette-cards on pavement, both quite clean Curious Beaks.

March 9th.—Cannot hear of a house-parlourmaid. Ethel, on the other hand, can hear of at least a hundred situations, and opulent motor-cars constantly dash up to front door, containing applicants for her services. Cook more and more unsettled. If this goes on, shall go to London and stay with Rose, in order to visit Agencies.

Meet Barbara, wearing new tweed, in

village this morning—nice bright girl, but long to suggest she should have adenoids removed. She says, Will I be an Angel and look in on her mother, now practically an invalid? I reply warmly Of course I will, not really meaning it, but remember that we are now in Lent and suddenly decide to go at once. Admire the new tweed. Barbara says It *is* rather nice, isn't it, and adds—a little strangely—that it came out of John Barker's Sale Catalogue, under four guineas, and only needed letting out at the waist and taking in a bit on the shoulders. Especially, she adds elliptically, now that skirts are longer again.

Barbara goes to Evening Service, and I go to look in on her mother, whom I find in shawls, sitting in an armchair reading—rather ostentatiously—enormous *Life of Lord Beaconsfield*. I ask how she is, and she shakes her head and enquires if I should ever guess that her pet name amongst her friends once used to be Butterfly? (This kind of question always so difficult, as either affirmative or negative reply apt to sound unsympathetic. Feel it would hardly do to suggest that Chrysalis, in view of the shawls, would now be more appropriate.) However, says Mrs. Blenkinsop with a sad smile, it is never her way to dwell upon herself and her own troubles. She just sits there, day after day, always ready to sympathise in the little joys and troubles of others, and I would hardly believe how unfailingly these are brought to her. People say, she adds deprecatingly, that just her Smile does them good. She does not know, she says, what they mean. (Neither do I.)

After this, there is a pause, and I feel that Mrs. B. is waiting for me to pour out my little joys and troubles. Perhaps she hopes that Robert has been unfaithful to me, or that I have fallen in love with the Vicar.

Am unable to rise to the occasion, so begin instead to talk about Barbara's new tweed. Mrs. Blenkinsop at once replies that, for her part, she has never given up all those little feminine touches that make All the

Difference. A ribbon here, a flower there. This leads to a story about what was once said to her by a friend, beginning "It's so wonderful, dear Mrs. Blenkinsop, to see the trouble you always take on behalf of others", and ending with Mrs. B.'s own reply, to the effect that she is only A Useless Old Woman, but that she has many, many friends, and that this must be because her motto has always been: Look Out and Not In: Look Up and not Down: Lend a Hand.

Conversation again languishes, and I have recourse to *Lord Beaconsfield*. What, I ask, does Mrs. B. feel about him? She feels, Mrs. B. replies, that he was a most Remarkable Personality. People have often said to Mrs. B., Ah, how lonely it must be for you, alone here, when dear Barbara is out enjoying herself with other young things. But Mrs. B.'s reply to this is No, no. She is never alone when she has Her Books. Books, to her, are *Friends*. Give her Shakespeare or Jane Austen, Meredith or Hardy, and she is Lost— lost in a world of her own. She sleeps so little

that most of her nights are spent in reading.
Have I any idea, asks Mrs. B., what it is like
to hear every hour, every half-hour, chiming out all through the night? I have no idea
whatever, since am invariably obliged to
struggle with overwhelming sleepiness from
nine o'clock onwards, but do not like to tell
her this, so take my departure. Mrs. B.'s
parting observation is an expression of
thanks to me for coming to enquire after
an old woman, and she is as well as she can
hope to be, at sixty-six years old—she
should say, sixty-six years *young*, all her
friends tell her.

Reach home totally unbenefited by this
visit, and with strange tendency to snap at
everybody I meet.

March 10*th.* — Still no house-parlourmaid, and write to ask Rose if I can go to
her for a week. Also write to old Aunt Gertrude in Shropshire to enquire if I may send
Vicky and Mademoiselle there on a visit, as
this will make less work in house while we

are short-handed. Do not, however, give Aunt Gertrude this reason for sending them. Ask Robert if he will be terribly lonely, and he says Oh no, he hopes I shall enjoy myself in London. Spend a great deal of eloquence explaining that I am *not* going to London to enjoy myself, but experience sudden fear that I am resembling Mrs. Blenkinsop, and stop abruptly.

Robert says nothing.

March 11th.—Rose wires that she will be delighted to put me up. Cook, very unpleasantly, says, "I'm sure I hope you'll enjoy your holiday, mum." Am precluded from making the kind of reply I should *like* to make, owing to grave fears that she should also give notice. Tell her instead that I hope to "get settled" with a house-parlourmaid before my return. Cook looks utterly incredulous and says she is sure she hopes so too, because really, things have been so unsettled lately. Pretend not to hear this and leave the kitchen.

Look through my clothes and find that I have nothing whatever to wear in London. Read in *Daily Mirror* that all evening dresses are worn long, and realise with horror that not one of mine comes even half-way down my legs.

March 12th.—Collect major portion of my wardrobe and dispatch to address mentioned in advertisement pages of *Time and Tide* as prepared to pay Highest Prices for Outworn Garments, cheque by return. Have gloomy foreboding that six penny stamps by return will more adequately represent value of my contribution, and am thereby impelled to add Robert's old shooting-coat, mackintosh dating from 1907, and least reputable woollen sweater. Customary struggle ensues between frank and straightforward course of telling Robert what I have done, and less straightforward, but more practical, decision to keep complete silence on the point and let him make discovery for himself after parcel has left the house. Conscience, as usual, is defeated, but nevertheless unsilenced.

(Query: Would it not indicate greater strength of character, even if lesser delicacy of feeling, not to spend so much time on regretting errors of judgement and of behaviour? Reply almost certainly in the affirmative. Brilliant, but nebulous, outline of powerful Article for *Time and Tide* here suggests itself: *Is Ruthlessness more Profitable than Repentance?* Failing article—for which time at the moment is lacking, owing to departure of house-parlourmaid and necessity of learning "Wreck of the Hesperus" to recite at Village Concert—would this make suitable subject for Debate at Women's Institute? Feel doubtful as to whether our Vicar's wife would not think subject-matter trenching upon ground more properly belonging to our Vicar.)

Resign from Book of the Month Club, owing to wide and ever-increasing divergence of opinion between us as to merits or demerits of recently published fiction. Write them long and eloquent letter about this, but remember after it is posted that I still owe them twelve shillings and sixpence for Maurois's *Byron*.

March 13th.—Vicky and Mademoiselle leave, in order to pay visit to Aunt Gertrude. Mademoiselle becomes sentimental and says, "Ah, déjà je languis pour notre retour!" As total extent of her absence at this stage is about half-an-hour, and they have three weeks before them, feel that this is not a spirit to be encouraged. See them into the train, when Mademoiselle at once produces eau-de-Cologne in case either, or both, should be ill, and come home again. House resembles the tomb, and the gardener says that Miss Vicky seems such a little bit of a thing to be sent right away like that, and it isn't as if she could write and *tell* me how she was getting on, either.

Go to bed feeling like a murderess.

March 14th.—Rather inadequate Postal

Order arrives, together with white tennis coat trimmed with rabbit, which—says accompanying letter—is returned as being unsaleable. Should like to know *why*. Toy with idea of writing to *Time and Tide*'s Editor, enquiring if every advertisement is subjected to personal scrutiny before insertion, but decide that this, in the event of a reply, might involve me in difficult explanations and diminish my *prestige* as occasional recipient of First Prize (divided) in Weekly Competition.

(*Mem.*: See whether tennis coat could be dyed and transformed into evening cloak.)

Am unfortunately found at home by callers, Mr. and Mrs. White, who are starting a Chicken-farm in the neighbourhood, and appear to have got married on the expectation of making a fortune out of it. We talk about chickens, houses, scenery, and the train-service between here and London. I ask if they play tennis, and politely suggest that both are probably brilliant performers. Mr. White staggers me by replying Oh, he wouldn't say *that*, exactly—meaning that he would, if it didn't seem like boasting. He enquires about Tournaments. Mrs. White is reminded of Tournaments in which they have, or have not, come out victors in the past. They refer to their handicap. Resolve never to ask the Whites to play on our extremely inferior court.

Later on talk about politicians. Mr. White says that in *his* opinion Lloyd George is clever, but Nothing Else. That's *all*, says Mr. White impressively. Just Clever. I refer to Coalition Government and Insurance Act, but Mr. White repeats firmly that both were brought about by mere Cleverness. He adds that Baldwin is a thoroughly *honest* man, and that Ramsay MacDonald is *weak*. Mrs. White supports him with an irrelevant statement to the effect that the Labour Party must be hand in glove with Russia, otherwise how would the Bolshevists dare to go on like that?

She also suddenly adds that Prohibition and the Jews and Everything are really the thin end of the wedge, don't I think so? I say Yes, I do, as the quickest way of ending the conversation, and ask if she plays the piano, to which she says No, but the Ukelele a little bit, and we talk about local shops and the delivery of a Sunday paper.

(*N.B.* Amenities of conversation afford very, very curious study sometimes, especially in the country.)

The Whites take their departure. Hope never to set eyes on either of them again.

March 15th.—Robert discovers absence of mackintosh dating from 1907. Says that he would "rather have lost a hundred pounds"—which I know to be untrue. Unsuccessful evening follows. Cannot make up my mind whether to tell him at once about shooting-coat and sweater, and get it all over in one, or leave him to find out for himself when present painful impression has had time to die away. Ray of light pierces impenetrable gloom when Robert is driven to enquire if I can tell him "a word for *calmer* in seven letters" and I, after some thought, suggest "*serener*"— which he says will do, and returns to *Times* Crossword Puzzle. Later he asks for famous mountain in Greece, but does not accept my too-hasty offer of Mount Atlas, nor listen to interesting explanation as to associative links between Greece, Hercules, and Atlas, which I proffer. After going into it at some length, I perceive that Robert is not attending, and retire to bed.

March 17th.—Travel up to London with Barbara Blenkinsop—(wearing new tweed) —who says she is going to spend a fortnight with old school-friend at Streatham and is looking forward to the Italian Art Exhibition. I say that I am, too, and ask after Mrs. B. Barbara says that she is Wonderful. We discuss Girl Guides, and exchange surmises as to reason why Mrs. T. at the Post Office is no longer on speaking terms with Mrs. L. at the shop. Later on, conversation takes a more intellectual turn, and we agree that the Parish Magazine needs Brightening Up. I suggest a cross-word puzzle, and Barbara says a Children's Page. Paddington is reached just as we decide that it would be hopeless to try and get a contribution to the Parish Magazine from anyone really *good*, such as Shaw, Bennett, or Galsworthy.

I ask Barbara to tea at my club one day next week, she accepts, and we part.

Met by Rose, who has a new hat, and says that *no one* is wearing a brim, which discourages me—partly because I have nothing *but* brims, and partly because I know only too well that I shall look my worst without one. Confide this fear to Rose, who says, Why not go to well-known Beauty Culture Establishment, and have course of treatment there? I look at myself in the glass, see much room for improvement, and agree to this, only stipulating that all shall be kept secret as the grave, as could not tolerate the idea of Lady B.'s comments, should she ever come to hear of it. Make appointment by telephone. In the meantime, says Rose, what about the Italian Art Exhibition? She herself has already been four times. I say Yes, yes—it is one of the things I have come to London *for*, but should prefer to go earlier in the day. Then, says Rose, the first thing to-morrow morning? To this I reply, with every sign of reluctance, that to-morrow morning *must* be devoted to Registry Offices. Well, says Rose, when *shall* we go? Let us, I urge, settle that a little later on, when I know better what I am doing. Can see that Rose thinks anything but well of me, but she is too tactful to say more. Quite realise that I shall have to go to the Italian Exhibition sooner or later, and am indeed quite determined to do so, but feel certain that I shall understand nothing about it when I do get there, and shall find myself involved in terrible difficulties when asked my impressions afterwards.

Rose's cook, as usual, produces marvellous dinner, and I remember with shame and compassion that Robert, at home, is sitting down to minced beef and macaroni cheese, followed by walnuts.

Rose says that she is taking me to dinner to - morrow, with distinguished woman-writer who has marvellous collection of Jade, to meet still more distinguished Professor (female) and others. Decide to go and buy an evening dress to-morrow, regardless of overdraft.

March 18*th.*—Very successful day, although Italian Art Exhibition still unvisited. (*Mem.*: Positively *must* go there before meeting Barbara for tea at my club.)

Visit several Registry Offices, and am told that maids do not like the country—which I know already—and that the wages I am offering are low. Come away from there depressed, and decide to cheer myself up by purchasing evening dress—which

I cannot afford—with present-day waist—
which does not suit me. Select the Bromp-
ton Road, as likely to contain what I want,
and crawl up it, scrutinising windows. Come
face-to-face with Barbara Blenkinsop, who
says, *How* extraordinary we should meet
here, to which I reply that that is so often the
way, when one comes to London. She is,
she tells me, just on her way to the Italian
Exhibition. . . . I at once say Good-bye, and
plunge into elegant establishment with expensive-looking garments in the window.

Try on five dresses, but find judgement of
their merits very difficult, as hair gets wilder
and wilder, and nose more devoid of powder.
Am also worried by extraordinary and tactless tendency of saleswoman to emphasise
the fact that all the colours I like are very
trying by daylight, but will be less so at
night. Finally settle on silver tissue with
large bow, stipulate for its immediate delivery, am told that this is impossible, reluctantly agree to carry it away with me in
cardboard box, and go away wondering if

it wouldn't have been better to choose the black chiffon instead.

Hope that Beauty Parlour experiment may enhance self-respect, at present at rather low ebb, but am cheered by going into Fuller's and sending boxes of chocolates to Robin and Vicky respectively. Add peppermint creams for Mademoiselle by an afterthought, as otherwise she may find herself *blessée*. Lunch on oxtail soup, lobster mayonnaise, and cup of coffee, as being menu furthest removed from that obtainable at home.

Beauty Parlour follows. Feel that a good deal could be written on this experience, and even contemplate—in connection with recent observations exchanged between Barbara B. and myself—brightening the pages of our Parish Magazine with result of my reflections, but on second thoughts abandon this, as unlikely to appeal to the Editor (Our Vicar).

Am received by utterly terrifying person with dazzling complexion, indigo-blue hair, and orange nails, presiding over reception room downstairs, but eventually passed on to extremely pretty little creature with auburn bob and charming smile. Am reassured. Am taken to discreet curtained cubicle and put into long chair. Subsequent operations, which take hours and hours, appear to consist of the removal of hundreds of layers of dirt from my face. (These discreetly explained away by charming operator as the result of "acidity".) She also plucks away portions of my eyebrows. Very, very painful operation.

Eventually emerge more or less unrecognisable, and greatly improved. Lose my head, and buy Foundation Cream, rouge, powder, lip-stick. Foresee grave difficulty in reconciling Robert to the use of these appliances, but decide not to think about this for the present.

Go back to Rose's flat in time to dress for dinner. She tells me that she spent the afternoon at the Italian Exhibition.

March 19th.—Rose takes me to dine with talented group of her friends, connected with Feminist Movement. I wear new frock, and for once in my life am satisfied with my appearance (but still regret great-aunt's diamond ring, now brightening pawnbroker's establishment back-street Plymouth). Am, however, compelled to make strong act of will in order to banish all recollection of bills that will subsequently come in from Beauty Parlour and dressmaker. Am able to succeed in this largely owing to charms of distinguished Feminists, all as kind as possible. Well-known Professor—(concerning whom I have previously consulted Rose as to the desirability of reading up something about Molecules or other kindred topic, for conversational purposes)—completely overcomes me by producing, with a charming smile, two cigarette-cards, as she has heard that I collect them for Robin. After this, throw all idea of Molecules to the winds, and am happier for the rest of the evening in consequence.

Editor of well-known literary weekly also present, and actually remembers that we met before at Literary Club dinner. I discover, towards the end of the dinner, that she has *not* visited the Italian Exhibition— and give Rose a look that I hope she takes to heart.

Cocktails, and wholly admirable dinner, further brighten the evening. I sit next Editor, and she rather rashly encourages me to give my opinion of her paper. I do so freely, thanks to cocktail and Editor's charming manners, which combine to produce in me the illusion that my words are witty, valuable, and thoroughly well worth listening to. (Am but too well aware that later in the night I shall wake up in cold sweat, and view this scene in retrospect with very different feelings as to my own part in it.)

Rose and I take our leave just before midnight, sharing taxi with very well-known woman dramatist. (Should much like Lady B. to know this, and have every intention of making casual mention to her of it at earliest possible opportunity.)

March 20*th.*—More Registry Offices, less success than ever.

Barbara Blenkinsop comes to tea with me at my club, and says that Streatham is very gay, and that her friends took her to a dance last night and a Mr. Crosbie Carruthers drove her home afterwards in his car. We then talk about clothes—dresses all worn long in the evening—this graceful, but not hygienic—women will never again submit to long skirts in the day-time—most people growing their hair—but eventually Barbara reverts to Mr. C. C. and asks if I think a girl makes herself cheap by allowing a man friend to take her out to dinner in Soho? I say No, not at all, and inwardly decide that Vicky would look nice as bridesmaid in blue taffetas, with little wreath of Banksia roses.

A letter from dear Robin, forwarded from home, arrives to-night. He says, wouldn't a motor tour in the Easter holidays be great fun, and a boy at school called Briggs is going on one. (Briggs is the only son of millionaire parents, owning two Rolls-Royces and any number of chauffeurs.) Feel that it would be unendurable to refuse this trustful request, and decide that I can probably persuade Robert into letting me drive the children to the far side of the county in the old Standard. Can call this modest expedition a motor tour if we stay the night at a pub. and return the next day.

At the same time realise that, financial situation being what it is, and moreover time rapidly approaching when great-aunt's diamond ring must either be redeemed, or relinquished for ever, there is nothing for it but to approach Bank on subject of an overdraft.

Am never much exhilarated at this prospect, and do not in the least find that it becomes less unpleasant with repetition, but rather the contrary. Experience customary difficulty in getting to the point, and Bank Manager and I discuss weather, political situation, and probable Starters for the Grand National with passionate suavity for some time. Inevitable pause occurs, and we look at one another across immense expanse of pink blotting-paper. Irrelevant impulse rises in me to ask if he has other supply, for use, in writing-table drawer, or if fresh pad is brought in whenever a client calls. (Strange divagations of the human brain under the stress of extreme nervousness presents itself here as interesting topic for speculation. Should like to hear opinion of Professor met last night on this point. Subject far preferable to Molecules.)

Long, and rather painful, conversation follows. Bank Manager kind, but if he says the word "security" once, he certainly says it twenty times. Am, myself, equally insistent with "temporary accommodation only", which I think sounds thoroughly business-like, and at the same time optimistic as to speedy repayment. Just as I think we are over the worst, Bank Manager reduces me to spiritual pulp by suggesting that we should see how the Account Stands at the Moment. Am naturally compelled to agree to this with air of well-bred and detached amusement, but am in reality well aware that the Account Stands—or, more accurately, totters—on a Debit Balance of Thirteen Pounds, two shillings, and tenpence. Large sheet of paper, bearing this impressive statement, is presently brought in and laid before us.

Negotiations resumed.

Eventually emerge into the street with purpose accomplished, but feeling completely unstrung for the day. Rose is kindness personified, produces Bovril and an excellent lunch, and agrees with me that it is All Nonsense to say that Wealth wouldn't mean Happiness, because we know quite well that it *would*.

March 21*st*.—Express to Rose serious fear that I shall lose my reason if no house-parlourmaid materialises. Rose, as usual, sympathetic, but can suggest nothing that I have not already tried. We go to a Sale in order to cheer ourselves up, and I buy yellow linen tennis-frock—£1 9s. 6d.—on strength of newly-arranged overdraft, but subsequently suffer from the conviction that I am taking the bread out of the mouths of Robin and Vicky.

Rather painful moment occurs when I suggest the Italian Exhibition to Rose, who replies—after a peculiar silence—that it is now *over*. Can think of nothing whatever to say, and do not care for dear Rose's expression, so begin at once to discuss new novels with as much intelligence as I can muster.

March 22nd.—Completely amazed by laconic postcard from Robert to say that local Registry Office can supply us with house-parlour*man*, and if I am experiencing difficulty in finding anyone, had we not better engage him? I telegraph back Yes, and then feel that I have made a mistake, but Rose says No, and refuses to let me rush out and telegraph again, for which, on subsequent calmer reflection, I feel grateful to her—and am sure that Robert would be still more so, owing to well-authenticated masculine dislike of telegrams.

Spend the evening writing immense letter to Robert enclosing list of duties of house-parlourman. (Jib at thought of being called by him in the mornings with early tea, and consult Rose, who says boldly, Think of waiters in Foreign Hotels!— which I do, and am reminded at once of many embarrassing episodes which I would rather forget.) Also send detailed instructions to Robert regarding the announcement of this innovation to Cook. Rose again takes up modern and fearless attitude, and says that Cook, mark her words, will be delighted.

I spend much of the night thinking over the whole question of running the house successfully, and tell myself—not by any

HOWARD FITZSIMMONS.

"HE DID IT, SHE SAYS, AT THE ZOO."

means for the first time—that my abilities are very, very deficient in this direction. Just as the realisation of this threatens to overwhelm me altogether, I fall asleep.

March 25th.—Return home, to Robert, Helen Wills, and new house-parlourman, who is—I now learn for the first time—named Fitzsimmons. I tell Robert that it is impossible that he should be called this. Robert replies, Why not? Can only say that if Robert cannot see this for himself, explanation will be useless. Then, says Robert, no doubt we can call him by his first name. This, on investigation, turns out to be Howard. Find myself quite unable to cope with any of it, and the whole situation is met by my never calling the house-parlourman anything at all except "you" and speaking of him to Robert as "Howard Fitzsimmons", in inverted commas as though intending to be funny. Very unsatisfactory solution.

Try to tell Robert all about London—

(with exception of Italian Exhibition, which I do not mention)—but Aladdin lamp flares up, which interferes, and have also to deal with correspondence concerning Women's Institute Monthly Meeting, replacement of broken bedroom tumblers—attributed to Ethel—disappearance of one pyjama-jacket and two table-napkins in the wash, and instructions to Howard Fitzs. concerning his duties. (*Mem.*: Must certainly make it crystal-clear that acceptable formula, when receiving an order, is not "Right-oh!" Cannot, at the moment, think how to word this, but must work it out, and then deliver with firmness and precision.)

Robert very kind about London, but perhaps rather more interested in my having met Barbara Blenkinsop—which, after all, I can do almost any day in the village—than in my views on *Nine till Six* (the best play I have seen for ages) or remarkable increase of traffic in recent years. Tell Robert by degrees about my new clothes. He asks when I expect to wear them, and I reply that one never knows—which is only too true—and conversation closes.

Write long letter to Angela, for the express purpose of referring casually to Rose's distinguished friends, met in London.

March 27th.—Angela replies to my letter, but says little about distinguished society in which I have been moving, and asks for full account of my impressions of Italian Exhibition. She and William, she says, went up on purpose to see it, and visited it three times. Can only say—but do not, of course, do so—that William must have been dragged there by the hair of his head.

March 28th.—Read admirable, but profoundly discouraging, article in *Time and Tide* relating to Bernard Shaw's women, but applying to most of us. Realise—not for the first time—that intelligent women can perhaps best perform their duty towards their own sex by devastating process of telling them the truth about themselves. At the same time, cannot feel that I shall really enjoy hearing it. Ultimate paragraph of article, moreover, continues to haunt me most unpleasantly with reference to own undoubted vulnerability where Robin and Vicky are concerned. Have very often wondered if Mothers are not rather A Mistake altogether, and now definitely come to the conclusion that they *are*.

Interesting speculation as to how they might best be replaced interrupted by necessity of seeing that Fitzs. is turning out spare-bedroom according to instructions. Am unspeakably disgusted at finding him sitting in spare-room armchair, with feet on the window-sill. He says that he is "not feeling very well". Am much more taken aback than he is, and lose my head to the extent of replying: "Then go and be it in your own room." Realise afterwards that this might have been better worded.

April 2nd.—Barbara calls. Can she, she

says, speak to me in *confidence?* I assure her
that she can, and at once put Helen Wills
and kitten out of the window in order to
establish confidential atmosphere. Sit, seething with excitement, in the hope that I
am at least going to be told that Barbara is
engaged. Try to keep this out of sight, and
to maintain expression of earnest and sympathetic attention only, whilst Barbara says
that it is sometimes very difficult to know
which way Duty lies, that she has always
thought a true woman's highest vocation is
home-making, and that the love of a Good
Man is the crown of life. I say Yes, Yes, to
all of this. (Discover, on thinking it over,
that I do not agree with any of it, and am
shocked at my own extraordinary duplicity.)

Barbara at length admits that Crosbie
has asked her to marry him—he did it, she
says, at the Zoo—and go out with him as
his wife to the Himalayas. This, says Barbara, is where all becomes difficult. She may
be old-fashioned—no doubt she is—but
can she leave her mother alone? No, she

cannot. Can she, on the other hand, give up dear Crosbie, who has never loved a girl before, and says that he never will again? No, she cannot.

Barbara weeps. I kiss her. Howard Fitzsimmons selects this moment to walk in with the tea, at which I sit down again in confusion and begin to talk about the Vicarage daffodils being earlier than ours, just as Barbara launches into the verdict in the Podmore Case. We gyrate uneasily in and out of these topics while Howard Fitzsimmons completes his preparations for tea. Atmosphere ruined, and destruction completed by my own necessary enquiries as to Barbara's wishes in the matter of milk, sugar, bread-and-butter, and so on. (*Mem.*: Must speak to Cook about sending in minute segment of sponge-cake, remains of one which, to my certain recollection, made its first appearance more than ten days ago. Also, why perpetual and unappetising procession of small rock-cakes?)

Robert comes in, he talks of swine-fever,

all further confidences become impossible. Barbara takes her leave immediately after tea, only asking if I could look in on her mother and have a Little Talk? I reluctantly agree to do so, and she mounts her bicycle and rides off. Robert says, That girl holds herself well, but it's a pity she has those ankles.

April 4th.—Go to see old Mrs. Blenkinsop. She is, as usual, swathed in shawls, but has exchanged *Lord Beaconsfield* for *Froude and Carlyle.* She says that I am very good to come and see a poor old woman, and that she often wonders how it is that so many of the younger generation seem to find their way to her by instinct. Is it, she suggests, because her *heart* has somehow kept young, in spite of her grey hair and wrinkles, ha-ha-ha, and so she has always been able to find the Silver Lining, she is thankful to say. I circuitously approach the topic of Barbara. Mrs. B. at once says that the young are very hard and selfish. This is natural, perhaps, but it saddens her. Not on her own account — no, no, no — but because she cannot bear to think of what Barbara will have to suffer from remorse when it is Too Late.

Feel a strong inclination to point out that this is *not* finding the Silver Lining, but refrain. Long monologue from old Mrs. B. follows. Main points that emerge are: (*a*) That Mrs. B. has not got very many more years to spend amongst us; (*b*) that all her life has been given up to others, but that she deserves no credit for this, as it is just the way she is made; (*c*) that all she wants is to see her Barbara happy, and it matters nothing at all that she herself should be left alone and helpless in her old age, and no one is to give a thought to that for a moment. Finally, that it has never been her way to think of herself or of her own feelings. People have often said to her that they believe she *has* no self—simply, none at all.

Pause, which I do not attempt to fill, ensues.

We return to Barbara, and Mrs. B. says it is very natural that a girl should be wrapped up in her own little concerns. I feel that we are getting no further, and boldly introduce the name of Crosbie Carruthers. Terrific effect on Mrs. B., who puts her hand on her heart, leans back, and begins to gasp and turn blue. She is sorry, she pants, to be so foolish, but it is now many nights since she has had any sleep at all, and the strain is beginning to tell. I must forgive her. I hastily do forgive her, and depart.

Very, very unsatisfactory interview.

Am told, on my way home, by Mrs. S. of the *Cross and Keys*, that a gentleman is staying there who is said to be engaged to Miss Blenkinsop, but the old lady won't hear of it, and he seems such a nice gentleman too, though perhaps not quite as young as some, and do I think the Himalayas would be All Right if there was a baby coming along? Exchange speculations and comments with Mrs. S. for some time before recollecting that the whole thing is supposed to be private, and that in any case gossip is undesirable.

Am met at home by Mademoiselle with intelligent enquiry as to the prospects of Miss Blenkinsop's immediate marriage, and the attitude adopted by old Mrs. B. "Le cœur d'une mère," says Mademoiselle sentimentally. Even the infant Vicky suddenly demands if that gentleman at the *Cross and Keys* is really Miss Blenkinsop's True Love? At this, Mademoiselle screams, "Ah, mon Dieu, ces enfants anglais!" and is much upset at impropriety of Vicky's language.

Even Robert enquires What All This Is, about Barbara Blenkinsop? I explain, and he returns—very, very briefly—that old Mrs. Blenkinsop ought to be Shot—which gets us no further, but meets with my entire approval.

April 10th.—Entire parish now seething with the *affaire* Blenkinsop. Old Mrs. B. falls ill, and retires to bed. Barbara bicycles madly up and down between her mother

and the garden of the *Cross and Keys*, where
C. C. spends much time reading copies of
The Times of India and smoking small
cigars. We are all asked by Barbara What
she Ought to Do, and all give different
advice. Deadlock appears to have been
reached, when C. C. suddenly announces
that he is summoned to London and must
have an answer One Way or the Other
immediately.

Old Mrs. B.—who has been getting better
and taking Port—instantly gets worse again
and says that she will not long stand in the
way of dear Barbara's happiness.

Period of fearful stress sets in, and Barbara and C. C. say Good-bye in the front
sitting-room of the *Cross and Keys*. They
have, says Barbara in tears, parted For
Ever, and Life is Over, and will I take the
Guides' Meeting for her to-night—which
I agree to do.

April 12*th*.—Return of Robin for the
holidays. He has a cold, and, as usual, is

short of handkerchiefs. I write to the Matron about this, but have no slightest hope of receiving either handkerchiefs or rational explanation of their disappearance. Robin mentions that he has invited "a boy" to come and stay for a week. I ask, Is he very nice and a great friend of yours? Oh no, says Robin, he is one of the most unpopular boys in the school. And after a moment he adds, *That's why*. Am touched, and think that this denotes a generous spirit, but am also undeniably rather apprehensive as to possible characteristics of future guest. I repeat the story to Mademoiselle, who—as usual, when I praise Robin—at once remarks: "Madame, notre petite Vicky n'a pas de défauts"—which is neither true nor relevant.

Receive a letter from Mary K. with postscript: Is it true that Barbara Blenkinsop is engaged to be married? and am also asked the same question by Lady B., who looks in on her way to some ducal function on the other side of the county. Have no time in which to enjoy being in the superior position of bestowing information, as Lady B. at once adds that *she* always advises girls to marry, no matter what the man is like, as any husband is better than none, and there are not nearly enough to go round.

I immediately refer to Rose's collection of distinguished Feminists, giving her to understand that I know them all well and intimately, and have frequently discussed the subject with them. Lady B. waves her hand—(in elegant white kid, new, not cleaned)—and declares That may be all very well, but if they could have got *husbands* they wouldn't *be* Feminists. I instantly assert that all have had husbands, and some two or three. This may or may not be true, but have seldom known stronger homicidal impulse. Final straw is added when Lady B. amiably observes that *I*, at least, have nothing to complain of, as she always thinks Robert such a safe, respectable husband for *any* woman. Give her briefly to understand that Robert is in reality a compound of Don Juan, the Marquis de Sade, and Dr. Crippen, but that we do not care to let it be known locally. Cannot say whether she is or is not impressed by this, as she declares herself obliged to go, because ducal function "cannot begin without her". All I can think of is to retort that Duchesses—(of whom, in actual fact, I do not know any)—always remind me of Alice in Wonderland, as do white kid gloves of the White Rabbit. Lady B. replies that I am always so well-read, and car moves off leaving her with, as usual, the last word.

Evolve in my own mind merry fantasy in which members of the Royal Family visit the neighbourhood and honour Robert and myself by becoming our guests at luncheon. (Cannot quite fit Howard Fitzs. into this scheme, but gloss over that aspect of the case.) Robert has just been raised to the peerage, and I am, with a slight and gracious inclination of the head, taking precedence of Lady B. at large dinner-party, when Vicky comes in to say that the Scissor-Grinder is at the door, and if we haven't anything to grind, he'll be pleased to attend to the clocks or rivet any china.

Am disconcerted at finding itinerant gipsy, of particularly low appearance, encamped at back door, with collection of domestic articles strewn all round him and his machine. Still more disconcerted at appearance of Mademoiselle, in fits of loud and regrettable Gallic merriment, bearing extremely unsuitable fragments of bedroom ware in either hand. . . . She, Vicky, and the Scissor-Grinder join in unseemly mirth, and I leave them to it, thankful that at least Lady B. is by now well on her way and cannot descend upon the scene. Am seriously exercised in my mind as to probable standard of humour with which Vicky will grow up.

Look for Robin and eventually find him with the cat, shut up into totally unventilated linen-cupboard, eating cheese which he says he found on the back stairs.

(Undoubtedly, a certain irony can be found in the fact that I have recently been appointed to new Guardians Committee, and am expected to visit Workhouse, etc., with particular reference to children's quarters, in order that I may offer valuable suggestions on questions of hygiene and general welfare of inmates. . . . Can only hope that fellow-members of the Committee will never be inspired to submit my own domestic arrangements to similar inspection.)

Write letters. Much interrupted by Helen Wills, wanting to be let out, kitten, wanting to be let in, and dear Robin, who climbs all over all the furniture, apparently unconscious that he is doing so, and tells me at the same time, loudly and in full, the story of *The Swiss Family Robinson.*

April 14*th.*—Cook electrifies me by asking me if I have heard that Miss Barbara Blenkinsop's engagement is on again, it's all over the village. The gentleman, she says, came down by the 8.45 last night, and is at

the *Cross and Keys*. As it is exactly 9.15
A.M. when she tells me this, I ask how she
knows? Cook merely repeats that It is All
Over the Village, and that Miss Barbara
will quite as like as not be married by
special licence, and old Mrs. B. is in such a
way as never was. Am disconcerted to find
that Cook and I have been talking our heads
off for the better part of forty minutes before I remember that gossip is both undignified and undesirable.

Just as I am putting on my hat to go down
to the Blenkinsops' our Vicar's wife rushes
in. All is true, she says, *and more*. Crosbie
Carruthers, in altogether desperate state,
has threatened suicide, and written terrific
farewell letter to Barbara, who has cried
herself—as our Vicar's wife rather strangely
expresses it—to the merest *pulp*, and begged
him to Come At Once. A Blenkinsop
Family Council has been summoned—old
Mrs. B. has had Attacks—(nobody quite
knows what of)—but has finally been per-
suaded to reconsider entire problem. Our

Vicar has been called in to give impartial advice and consolation to all parties. He is there now. Surely, I urge, he will use all his influence on behalf of C. C. and Barbara? Our Vicar's wife, agitated, says Yes, Yes,— he is all in favour of young folk living their own lives, whilst at the same time he feels that a mother's claims are sacred, and although he realises the full beauty of self-sacrifice, yet on the other hand no one knows better than he does that the devotion of a Good Man is not to be lightly relinquished.

Feel that if this is to be our Vicar's only contribution towards the solution of the problem, he might just as well have stayed at home—but naturally do not impart this opinion to his wife. We decide to walk down to the village, and do so. The gardener stops me on the way, and says he thought I might like to know that Miss Barbara's young gentleman has turned up again, and wants to marry her before he sails next month, and old Mrs. Blenkinsop is taking on so, they think she'll have a stroke.

Similar information also reaches us from six different quarters in the village. No less than three motor-cars and two bicycles are to be seen outside old Mrs. B.'s cottage, but no one emerges, and I am obliged to suggest that our Vicar's wife should come home with me to lunch. This she does, after many demurs, and gets cottage-pie—(too much onion) — rice-shape, and stewed prunes. Should have sent to the farm for cream, if I had known.

April 15th.—Old Mrs. Blenkinsop reported to have Come Round. Elderly unmarried female Blenkinsop, referred to as Cousin Maud, has suddenly materialised, and offered to live with her—Our Vicar has come out boldly in support of this scheme— and Crosbie Carruthers has given Barbara engagement ring with three stones, said to be rare Indian Topazes, and has gone up to town to Make Arrangements. Immediate announcement in the *Morning Post* expected.

April 18*th*.—Receive visit from Barbara, who begs that I will escort her to London for quiet and immediate wedding. Am obliged to refuse, owing to bad colds of Robin and Vicky, general instability of domestic staff, and customary unsatisfactory financial situation. Offer then passed on to our Vicar's wife, who at once accepts it. I undertake, however, at Barbara's urgent request, to look in as often as possible on her mother. Will I, adds Barbara, make it clear that she is not losing a Daughter, but only gaining a Son, and two years will soon be over, and at the end of that time dear Crosbie will bring her home to England. I recklessly commit myself to doing anything and everything, and write to the Army and Navy Stores for a luncheon-basket, to give as wedding-present to Barbara. The Girl Guides present her with a sugar-castor and a waste-paper basket embossed with raffia flowers. Lady B. sends a chafing-dish with a card bearing illegible and far-fetched joke connected with Indian

COUSIN MAUD.

CISSIE CRABBE.

curries. We all agree that this is not in the least amusing. Mademoiselle causes Vicky to present Barbara with small tray-cloth, on which two hearts are worked in cross-stitch.

April 19*th*.—Both children simultaneously develop incredibly low complaint known as "pink-eye" that everyone unites in telling me is peculiar to the more saliently neglected and underfed section of the juvenile population in the East End of London.

Vicky has a high temperature and is put to bed, while Robin remains on his feet, but is not allowed out of doors until present cold winds are over. I leave Vicky to Mademoiselle and *Les Mémoires d'un Âne* in the night-nursery, and undertake to amuse Robin downstairs. He says that he has a Splendid Idea. This turns out to be that I should play the piano, whilst he simultaneously sets off the gramophone, the musical-box, and the chiming clock.

I protest.

Robin implores, and says It will be just like an Orchestra. (Shade of Dame Ethel Smyth, whose Reminiscences I have just been reading!) I weakly yield, and attack, *con spirito*, "The Broadway Melody" in the key of C Major. Robin, in great excitement, starts the clock, puts "Mucking About the Garden" on the gramophone, and winds up the musical-box, which tinkles out the Waltz from *Floradora* in a tinny sort of way, and no recognisable key. Robin springs about and cheers. I watch him sympathetically and keep down, at his request, the loud pedal.

The door is flung open by Howard Fitzs., and Lady B. enters, wearing bran-new green Kasha with squirrel collar, and hat to match, and accompanied by military-looking friend.

Have no wish to record subsequent few minutes, in which I endeavour to combine graceful greetings to Lady B. and the military friend, with simple and yet digni-fied explanation of singular state of affairs

presented to them, and unobtrusive directions to Robin to switch off musical-box
and gramophone and betake himself and
his pink-eye upstairs. Clock has mercifully
ceased to chime, and Robin struggles
gallantly with musical-box, but "Mucking
About the Garden" continues to ring
brazenly through the room for what seems
about an hour and a half. . . . (Should not
have minded quite so much if it had been
"Classical Memories", which I also possess,
or even a Layton and Johnstone duet.)

Robin goes upstairs, but not until after
Lady B. has closely scrutinised him, and
observed that He looks like Measles, to her.
Military friend tactfully pretends absorp-
tion in the nearest bookcase until this is
over, when he emerges with breezy observation concerning *Bulldog Drummond*.

Lady B. at once informs him that he must
not say that kind of thing to *me*, as I am
so Very Literary. After this, the military
friend looks at me with unconcealed horror,
and does not attempt to speak to me again.

On the whole, am much relieved when the call is over.

Go upstairs and see Vicky, who seems worse, and telephone for the doctor. Mademoiselle begins lugubrious story, which is evidently destined to end disastrously, about a family in her native town mysteriously afflicted by Smallpox—(of which all the preliminary symptoms were identical with those of Vicky's present disorder)—afterwards traced to unconsidered purchase by *le papa* of Eastern rugs, sold by itinerant vendor on the quay at Marseilles. Cut her short after the death of the six-months-old baby, as I perceive that all the other five children are going to follow suit, as slowly and agonisingly as possible.

April 20th.—Vicky develops unmistakable measles, and doctor says that Robin may follow suit any day. Infection must have been picked up at Aunt Gertrude's, and shall write and tell her so.

Extraordinary and nightmare-like state

of affairs sets in, and I alternate between making lemonade for Vicky and telling her the story of *Frederick and the Picnic* upstairs, and bathing Robin's pink-eye with boracic lotion and reading *The Coral Island* to him downstairs.

Mademoiselle is *dévouée* in the extreme, and utterly refuses to let anyone but herself sleep in Vicky's room, but find it difficult to understand exactly on what principle it is that she persists in wearing a *peignoir* and *pantoufles* day and night alike. She is also unwearied in recommending very strange *tisanes*, which she proposes to brew herself from herbs—fortunately unobtainable—in the garden.

Robert, in this crisis, is less helpful than I could wish, and takes up characteristic-ally masculine attitude that We are All Making a Great Fuss about Very Little, and the whole thing has been got up for the express purpose of putting him to in-convenience—(which, however, it does not do, as he stays out all day, and insists on having dinner exactly the same as usual every evening).

Vicky incredibly and alarmingly good, Robin almost equally so in patches, but renders himself unpopular with Fitzs. by leaving smears of Plasticine, pools of paint-water, and even blots of ink on much of the furniture. Find it very difficult to combine daily close inspection of him, with a view to discovering the beginning of measles, with light-hearted optimism that I feel to be right and rational attitude of mind.

Weather very cold and rainy, and none of the fires will burn up. Cannot say why this is, but it adds considerably to condition of gloom and exhaustion which I feel to be gaining upon me hourly.

April 25th.—Vicky recovering slowly, Robin showing no signs of measles. Am myself victim of curious and unpleasant form of chill, no doubt due to over-fatigue.

Howard Fitzsimmons gives notice, to the relief of everyone, and I obtain service of superior temporary house-parlourmaid at cost of enormous weekly sum.

April 27th.—Persistence of chill compels me to retire to bed for half a day, and Robert suggests gloomily that I have caught the measles. I demonstrate that this is impossible, and after lunch get up and play cricket with Robin on the lawn. After tea, keep Vicky company. She insists upon playing at the Labours of Hercules, and we give energetic representations of slaughtering the Hydra, cleaning out the Augean Stables, and so on. Am divided between gratification at Vicky's classical turn of mind and strong disinclination for so much exertion.

May 7th.—Resume Diary after long and deplorable interlude, vanquished chill having suddenly reappeared with immense force and fury, and revealed itself as measles. Robin, on same day, begins to cough, and expensive hospital nurse materialises and takes complete charge. She proves kind and efficient, and brings me messages from the children, and realistic drawing from Robin entitled "Ill person being eaten up by jerms".

(*Query:* Is dear Robin perhaps future Heath Robinson or Arthur Watts?)

Soon after this all becomes incoherent and muddled. Chief recollection is of hearing the doctor say that of course my Age is against me, which hurts my feelings and makes me feel like old Mrs. Blenkinsop. After a few days, however, I get the better of my age, and am given champagne, grapes, and Valentine's Meat Juice.

Should like to ask what all this is going to cost, but feel it would be ungracious.

The children, to my astonishment, are up and about again, and allowed to come and see me. They play at Panthers on the bed, until removed by Nurse. Robin reads aloud to me, article on Lord Chesterfield from pages of *Time and Tide*, which has struck him because he, like the writer, finds it difficult to accept a compliment gracefully. What do *I* do, he enquires, when I receive so many compliments all at once that I am overwhelmed? Am obliged to admit that I have not yet found myself in this predicament, at which Robin looks surprised, and slightly disappointed.

Robert, the nurse, and I decide in conclave that the children shall be sent to Bude for a fortnight with Nurse, and Mademoiselle given a holiday in which to recover from her exertions. I am to join the Bude party when doctor permits.

Robert goes to make this announcement to the nursery, and comes back with fatal news that Mademoiselle is *blessée*, and that the more he asks her to explain, the more monosyllabic she becomes. Am not allowed either to see her or to write explanatory and soothing note and am far from reassured by Vicky's report that Mademoiselle, bathing her, has wept, and said that in England there are hearts of stone.

May 12th.—Further interlude, this time owing to trouble with the eyes. (No doubt concomitant of my Age, once again.) The children and hospital nurse depart on the 9th, and I am left to gloomy period of total inactivity and lack of occupation. Get up after a time and prowl about in kind of semi-ecclesiastical darkness, further intensified by enormous pair of tinted spectacles. One and only comfort is that I cannot see myself in the glass. Two days ago, decide to make great effort and come down for tea, but nearly relapse and go straight back to bed again at sight of colossal demand for the Rates, confronting me on hall-stand without so much as an envelope between us.

(*Mem.*: This sort of thing so very unlike picturesque convalescence in a novel, when heroine is gladdened by sight of spring flowers, sunshine, and what not. No mention ever made of Rates, or anything like them.)

Miss the children very much and my chief companion is kitchen cat, a hard-bitten

animal with only three and a half legs
and a reputation for catching and eating a
nightly average of three rabbits. We get
on well together until I have recourse to
the piano, when he invariably yowls and
asks to be let out. On the whole, am obliged
to admit that he is probably right, for I
have forgotten all I ever knew, and am reduced to playing popular music by ear,
which I do badly.

Dear Barbara sends me a book of Loopy
Limericks, and Robert assures me that I
shall enjoy them later on. Personally, feel
doubtful of surviving many more days of
this kind.

May 13*th.*—Regrettable, but undeniable
ray of amusement lightens general murk on
hearing report, through Robert, that Cousin
Maud Blenkinsop possesses a baby Austin,
and has been seen running it all round the
parish with old Mrs. B., shawls and all, beside her. (It is many years since Mrs. B.
gave us all to understand that if she so much

as walked across the room unaided, she would certainly fall down dead.)

Cousin Maud, adds Robert thoughtfully, is not *his* idea of a good driver. He says no more, but I at once have dramatic visions of old Mrs. B. flying over the nearest hedge, shawls waving in every direction, while Cousin Maud and the baby Austin charge a steam-roller in a narrow lane. Am sorry to record that this leads to hearty laughter on my part, after which I feel better than for weeks past.

The doctor comes to see me, says that he *thinks* my eyelashes will grow again—(should have preferred something much more emphatic, but am too much afraid of further reference to my age to insist)—and agrees to my joining children at Bude next week. He also, reluctantly, and with an air of suspicion, says that I may use my eyes for an hour every day, unless pain ensues.

May 15th.—Our Vicar's wife, hearing that I am no longer in quarantine, comes to

enliven me. Greet her with an enthusiasm
to which she must, I fear, be unaccustomed,
as it appears to startle her. Endeavour to
explain it (perhaps a little tactlessly) by
saying that I have been alone so long . . .
Robert out all day . . . children at Bude . . .
and end up with quotation to the effect that
I never hear the sweet music of speech, and
start at the sound of my own. Can see by
the way our Vicar's wife receives this that
she does not recognise it as a quotation, and
believes the measles to have affected my
brain. (Query: Perhaps she is right?) More
normal atmosphere established by a plea
from our Vicar's wife that kitchen cat may
be put out of the room. It is, she knows,
very foolish of her, but the presence of a cat
makes her feel faint. Her grandmother was
exactly the same. Put a cat into the same
room as her grandmother, hidden under the
sofa if you liked, and in two minutes the
grandmother would say: "I believe there's
a cat in this room," and at once turn
queer. I hastily put kitchen cat out of the

window, and we agree that heredity is very odd.

And now, says our Vicar's wife, how am I? Before I can reply, she does so for me, and says that she knows just how I feel. Weak as a rat, legs like cotton-wool, no spine whatever, and head like a boiled owl. Am depressed by this diagnosis, and begin to feel that it must be correct. However, she adds, all will be different after a blow in the wind at Bude, and meanwhile, she must tell me all the news.

She does so.

Incredible number of births, marriages, and deaths appear to have taken place in the parish in the last four weeks; also Mrs. W. has dismissed her cook and cannot get another one, our Vicar has written a letter about Drains to the local paper and it has been put in, and Lady B. has been seen in a new car. To this our Vicar's wife adds rhetorically: Why not an aeroplane, she would like to know? (Why not, indeed?)

Finally a Committee Meeting has been

held—at which, she interpolates hastily, I was much missed—and a Garden Fête arranged, in aid of funds for Village Hall. It would be so nice, she adds optimistically, if the Fête could be held *here*. I agree that it would, and stifle a misgiving that Robert may not agree. In any case, he knows, and I know, and our Vicar's wife knows, that Fête will have to take place here, as there isn't anywhere else.

Tea is brought in—superior temporary's afternoon out, and Cook has, as usual, carried out favourite labour-saving device of three sponge-cakes and one bun jostling one another on the same plate—and we talk about Barbara and Crosbie Carruthers, bee-keeping, modern youth, and difficulty of removing oil-stains from carpets. Have I, asks our Vicar's wife, read *A Brass Hat in No Man's Land?* No, I have not. Then, she says, *don't*, on any account. There are so many sad and shocking things in life as it *is*, that writers should confine themselves to the bright, the happy, and the beautiful.

This the author of *A Brass Hat* has entirely failed to do. It subsequently turns out that our Vicar's wife has not read the book herself, but that our Vicar has skimmed it, and declared it to be very painful and unnecessary. (*Mem.*: Put *Brass Hat* down for *Times* Book Club list, if not already there.)

Our Vicar's wife suddenly discovers that it is six o'clock, exclaims that she is shocked, and attempts *fausse sortie*, only to return with urgent recommendation to me to try Valentine's Meat Juice, which once practically, under Providence, saved our Vicar's uncle's life. Story of the uncle's illness, convalescence, recovery, and subsequent death at the age of eighty-one, follows. Am unable to resist telling her, in return, about wonderful effect of Bemax on Mary Kellway's youngest, and this leads—curiously enough—to the novels of Anthony Trollope, death of the Begum of Bhopal, and scenery in the Lake Country.

At twenty minutes to seven, our Vicar's wife is again shocked, and rushes out of the house. She meets Robert on the doorstep and stops to tell him that I am as thin as a rake, and a very bad colour, and the eyes, after measles, often give rise to serious trouble. Robert, so far as I can hear, makes no answer to any of it, and our Vicar's wife finally departs.

(Query here suggests itself: Is not silence frequently more efficacious than the utmost eloquence? Answer probably yes. Must try to remember this more often than I do.)

Second post brings a long letter from Mademoiselle, recuperating with friends at Clacton-on-Sea, written, apparently, with a pin point dipped in violet ink on thinnest imaginable paper, and crossed in every direction. Decipher portions of it with great difficulty, but am relieved to find that I am still "Bien-chère Madame" and that recent mysterious affront has been condoned.

(*Mem.*: If Cook sends up jelly even once again, as being suitable diet for convalescence, shall send it straight back to the kitchen.)

May 16th.—But for disappointing children, should be much tempted to abandon scheme for my complete restoration to health at Bude. Weather icy cold, self feeble and more than inclined to feverishness, and Mademoiselle, who was to have come with me, and helped with children, now writes that she is *désolée*, but has developed *une angine*. Do not know what this is, and have alarming thoughts about Angina Pectoris, but dictionary reassures me. I say to Robert: "After all, shouldn't I get well just as quickly at home?" He replies briefly: "Better go," and I perceive that his mind is made up. After a moment he suggests—but without real conviction—that I might like to invite our Vicar's wife to come with me. I reply with a look only, and suggestion falls to the ground.

A letter from Lady B. saying that she has only just heard about measles—(Why only just, when news has been all over parish for weeks?) and is so sorry, especially as measles are no joke at my age—(Can she be in league with Doctor, who also used identical objectionable expression?). — She cannot come herself to enquire, as with so many visitors always coming and going it wouldn't be wise, but if I want anything from the House, I am to telephone without hesitation. She has given "her people" orders that anything I ask for is to be sent up. Have a very good mind to telephone and ask for a pound of tea and Lady B.'s pearl necklace —(Could Cleopatra be quoted as precedent here?)—and see what happens.

Further demand for the Rates arrives, and Cook sends up jelly once more for lunch. I offer it to Helen Wills, who gives one heave, and turns away. Feel that this would more than justify me in sending down entire dish untouched, but Cook will certainly give notice if I do, and cannot face possibility. Interesting to note that although by this time *all* Cook's jellies take away at sight what appetite measles have left me, am more wholly revolted by emerald green variety than by yellow or red. Should like to work out possible Freudian significance of this, but find myself unable to concentrate.

Go to sleep in the afternoon, and awake sufficiently restored to do what I have long contemplated and Go Through my clothes. Result so depressing that I wish I had never done it. Have nothing fit to wear, and if I had, should look like a scarecrow in it at present. Send off parcel with knitted red cardigan, two evening dresses (much too short for present mode), three out-of-date hats, and tweed skirt that bags at the knees, to Mary Kellway's Jumble Sale, where she declares that *anything* will be welcome. Make out a list of all the new clothes I require, get pleasantly excited about them, am again confronted with the Rates, and put the list in the fire.

May 17th.—Robert drives me to North Road station to catch train for Bude. Temperature has fallen again, and I ask Robert if it is below zero. He replies briefly and untruthfully that the day will get warmer as it goes on, and no doubt Bude will be one blaze of sunshine. We arrive early and sit on a bench on the platform next to a young woman with a cough, who takes one look at me and then says: "Dreadful, isn't it?" Cannot help feeling that she has summarised the whole situation quite admirably. Robert hands me my ticket—he has handsomely offered to make it first-class and I have refused—and gazes at me with rather strange expression. At last he says: "You don't think you're going there to *die*, do you?" Now that he suggests it, realise that I *do* feel very like that, but summon up smile that I feel to be unconvincing and make sprightly reference to Bishop, whose name I forget, coming to lay his bones at place the name of which I cannot remember. All of it appears to be Greek to Robert, and I leave him still trying to unravel it. Journey ensues and proves chilly and exhausting. Rain lashes at the windows, and every time carriage door opens—which is often—gust of icy wind, mysteriously blowing in two opposite directions at once, goes up my legs and down back of my neck. Have not told children by what train I am arriving, so no one meets me, not even bus on which I had counted. Am, however, secretly thankful, as this gives me an excuse for taking a taxi. Reach lodgings at rather uninspiring hour of 2.45, too early for tea or bed, which constitute present summit of my ambitions. Uproarious welcome from children, both in blooming health and riotous spirits, makes up for everything.

May 19*th*.—Recovery definitely in sight, although almost certainly retarded by landlady's inspiration of sending up a nice jelly for supper on evening of arrival. Rooms reasonably comfortable—(except for extreme cold, which is, says landlady, quite unheard-of at this or any other time of year) —all is linoleum, pink and gold china, and enlarged photographs of females in lace collars and males with long moustaches and bow ties. Robin, Vicky, and the hospital nurse—retained at vast expense as a temporary substitute for Mademoiselle—have apparently braved the weather and spent much time on the Breakwater. Vicky has also made friends with a little dog, whose name she alleges to be "Baby", a gentleman who sells papers, another gentleman who drives about in a Sunbeam, and the head waiter from the Hotel. I tell her about Mademoiselle's illness, and after a silence she says "Oh!" in tones of brassy indifference, and resumes topic of little dog "Baby". Robin, from whom I cannot help hoping better things, makes no comment except "Is she?" and immediately adds a request for a banana.

(*Mem.*: Would it not be possible to write more domesticated and less foreign version of *High Wind in Jamaica*, featuring extraordinary callousness of infancy?) Can distinctly recollect heated correspondence in *Time and Tide* regarding *vraisemblance* or otherwise of Jamaica children, and now range myself, decidedly and for ever, on the side of the author. Can quite believe that dear Vicky would murder any number of sailors, if necessary.

May 23rd.—Sudden warm afternoon, children take off their shoes and dash into pools, landlady says that it's often like this on the *last* day of a visit to the sea, she's noticed, and I take brisk walk over the cliffs, wearing thick tweed coat, and really begin to feel quite warm at the end of an hour. Pack suit-case after children are in bed, register resolution never to let stewed prunes and custard form part of any meal ever again as long as I live, and thankfully write postcard to Robert, announcing time of our arrival at home to-morrow.

May 28th.—Mademoiselle returns, and is greeted with enthusiasm—to my great relief. (Robin and Vicky perhaps less like Jamaica children than I had feared.) She has on new black and white check skirt, white blouse with frills, black kid gloves, embroidered in white on the backs, and black straw hat almost entirely covered in purple violets, and informs me that the whole outfit was made by herself at a total cost of one pound, nine shillings, and four-pence-halfpenny. The French undoubtedly thrifty, and gifted in using a needle, but cannot altogether stifle conviction that a shade less economy might have produced better results.

She presents me, in the kindest way, with a present in the shape of two blue glass flower-vases, of spiral construction, and adorned with gilt knobs at many unexpected points. Vicky receives a large artificial-silk red rose, which she fortunately appears to admire, and Robin a small affair in wire that is intended, says Mademoiselle, to extract the stones out of cherries.

(*Mem.*: Interesting to ascertain number of these ingenious contrivances sold in a year.)

Am privately rather overcome by Mademoiselle's generosity, and wish that we could reach the level of the French in what they themselves describe as *petits soins*. Place the glass vases in conspicuous position on dining-room mantelpiece, and am fortunately just in time to stem comment which I see rising to Robert's lips when he sits down to mid-day meal and perceives them.

After lunch, Robin is motored back to school by his father, and I examine Vicky's summer wardrobe with Mademoiselle, and find that she has outgrown everything she has in the world.

May 30th.—Arrival of *Time and Tide*, find that I have been awarded half of second prize for charming little effort that in my opinion deserves better. Robert's attempt receives an honourable mention. Recognise pseudonym of first-prize winner as being that adopted by Mary Kellway. Should like to think that generous satisfaction envelops me, at dear friend's success, but am not sure. This week's competition announces itself as a Triolet—literary form that I cannot endure, and rules of which I am totally unable to master.

Receive telephone invitation to lunch with the Frobishers on Sunday. I accept, less because I want to see them than because a change from domestic roast beef and gooseberry-tart always pleasant; moreover, absence makes work lighter for the servants. (*Mem.*: Candid and intelligent self-examination as to motive, etc., often leads to very distressing revelations.)

Constrained by conscience, and recollection of promise to Barbara, to go and call on old Mrs. Blenkinsop. Receive many kind enquiries in village as to my complete recovery from measles, but observe singular tendency on part of everybody else to treat this very serious affliction as a joke.

Find old Mrs. B.'s cottage in unheard-of condition of hygienic ventilation, no doubt attributable to Cousin Maud. Windows all wide open, and casement curtains flapping in every direction, very cold east wind more than noticeable. Mrs. B.—(surely fewer shawls than formerly?)—sitting quite close to open window, and not far from equally open door, seems to have turned curious shade of pale-blue, and shows tendency to shiver. Room smells strongly of furniture polish and black-lead. Fireplace, indeed, exhibits recent handsome application of the latter, and has evidently not held fire for days past. Old Mrs. B. more silent than of old, and makes no reference to silver linings and the like. (Can spirit of optimism have been blown away by living in continual severe draught?) Cousin Maud comes in almost immediately. Have met her once before, and say so, but she makes it clear that this encounter left no impression, and has entirely escaped her memory. Am convinced that Cousin Maud is one of those people who pride themselves on always speaking the truth. She is wearing brick-red sweater—feel sure she knitted it herself—tweed skirt, longer at the back than in front—and large row of pearl beads. Has very hearty and emphatic manner, and uses many slang expressions.

I ask for news of Barbara, and Mrs. B.— (voice a mere bleat, by comparison with Cousin Maud's)—says that the dear child will be coming down once more before she sails, and that continued partings are the lot of the Aged, and to be expected. I begin to hope that she is approaching her old form, but all is stopped by Cousin Maud, who shouts out that we're not to talk Rot, and it's a jolly good thing Barbara has got Off the Hooks at last, poor old girl. We then talk about golf handicaps, Roedean—Cousin Maud's dear old school—and the baby Austin. More accurate statement would perhaps be that Cousin Maud talks, and we listen. No sign of *Life of Disraeli*, or any other literary activities, such as old Mrs. B. used to be surrounded by, and do not like to enquire what she now does with her time. Disquieting suspicion that this is probably settled for her, without reference to her wishes.

Take my leave feeling depressed. Old Mrs. B. rolls her eyes at me as I say good-bye, and mutters something about not being here much longer, but this is drowned by hearty laughter from Cousin Maud, who declares that she is Nothing but an Old Humbug and will See Us All Out.

Am escorted to the front gate by Cousin Maud, who tells me what a topping thing it is for old Mrs. B. to be taken out of herself a bit, and asks if it isn't good to be Alive on a bracing day like this? Should like to reply that it would be far better for some of us to be dead, in my opinion, but spirit for this repartee fails me, and I weakly reply that I know what she means. I go away before she has time to slap me on the back, which I feel certain will be the next thing.

Had had in mind amiable scheme for writing to Barbara to-night to tell her that old Mrs. B. is quite wonderful, and showing no signs of depression, but this cannot now be done, and after much thought, do not write at all, but instead spend the evening trying to reconcile grave discrepancy between account - book, counterfoils of cheque-book, and rather unsympathetically worded communication from the Bank.

June 1st. — Sunday lunch with the Frobishers, and four guests staying in the house with them—introduced as, apparently, Colonel and Mrs. Brightpie—(which seems impossible)—Sir William Reddie— or Ready, or Reddy, or perhaps even Reddeigh—and My sister Violet. Latter quite astonishingly pretty, and wearing admirable flowered tussore that I, as usual, mentally try upon myself, only to realise that it would undoubtedly suggest melancholy saying concerning mutton dressed as lamb.

The Colonel sits next to me at lunch, and we talk about fishing, which I have never attempted, and look upon as cruelty to animals, but this, with undoubted hypocrisy and moral cowardice, I conceal. Robert has My sister Violet, and I hear him at intervals telling her about the pigs, which seems odd, but she looks pleased, so perhaps is interested.

Conversation suddenly becomes general, as topic of present-day Dentistry is introduced by Lady F. We all, except Robert, who eats bread, have much to say.

(*Mem.*: Remember to direct conversation into similar channel, when customary periodical deathly silence descends upon guests at my own table.)

Weather is wet and cold, and had confidently hoped to escape tour of the garden, but this is not to be, and directly lunch is over we rush out into the damp. Boughs drip on to our heads and water squelches beneath our feet, but rhododendrons and lupins undoubtedly very magnificent, and references to Ruth Draper not more numerous than usual. I find myself walking with Mrs. Brightpie (?), who evidently knows all that can be known about a garden. Fortunately she is prepared to originate all the comments herself, and I need only

say, "Yes, isn't that an attractive variety?"
and so on. She enquires once if I have *ever*
succeeded in making the dear blue Grandi-
flora Magnifica Superbiensis—(or something
like that)—feel really happy and at home
in this climate? to which I am able to reply
with absolute truth by a simple negative,
at which I fancy she looks rather relieved.
Is her own life perhaps one long struggle
to acclimatise the G. M. S.? and what would
she have replied if I had said that, in *my*
garden, the dear thing grew like a weed?

(*Mem.*: Must beware of growing tendency to indulge in similar idle speculations,
which lead nowhere, and probably often
give me the appearance of being absent-
minded in the society of my fellow-
creatures.)

After prolonged inspection, we retrace
steps, and this time find myself with Sir
William R. and Lady F. talking about
grass. Realise with horror that we are now
making our way towards the *stables*. Nothing whatever to be done about it, except

N

keep as far away from the horses as possible, and refrain from any comment whatever, in hopes of concealing that I know nothing about horses except that they frighten me. Robert, I notice, looks sorry for me, and places himself between me and terrifying-looking animal that glares out at me from loose-box and curls up its lip. Feel grateful to him, and eventually leave stables with shattered nerves and soaking wet shoes. Exchange customary graceful farewells with host and hostess, saying how much I have enjoyed coming.

(Query here suggests itself, as often before: Is it utterly impossible to combine the amenities of civilisation with even the minimum of honesty required to satisfy the voice of conscience? Answer still in abeyance at present.)

Robert goes to Evening Service, and I play Halma with Vicky. She says that she wants to go to school, and produces string of excellent reasons why she should do so. I say that I will think it over, but am aware, by previous experience, that Vicky has almost miraculous aptitude for getting her own way, and will probably succeed in this instance as in others.

Rather depressing Sunday supper—cold beef, baked potatoes, salad, and depleted cold tart—after which I write to Rose, the Cleaners, the Army and Navy Stores, and the County Secretary of the Women's Institute, and Robert goes to sleep over the *Sunday Pictorial*.

June 3rd.—Astounding and enchanting change in the weather, which becomes warm. I carry chair, writing-materials, rug, and cushion into the garden, but am called in to have a look at the Pantry Sink, please, as it seems to have blocked itself up. Attempted return to garden frustrated by arrival of note from the village concerning Garden Fête arrangements, which requires immediate answer, necessity for speaking to the butcher on the telephone, and sudden realisation that Laundry List hasn't yet been made out, and the Van will be here at eleven. When it does come, I have to speak about the tablecloths, which leads—do not know how—to long conversation about the Derby, the Van speaking highly of an outsider—*Trews*—whilst I uphold the chances of *Silver Flare*—(mainly because I like the name).

Shortly after this, Mrs. S. arrives from the village, to collect jumble for Garden Fête, which takes time. After lunch, sky clouds over, and Mademoiselle and Vicky kindly help me to carry chair, writing-materials, rug, and cushion into the house again.

Robert receives letter by second post announcing death of his godfather, aged ninety-seven, and decides to go to the funeral on 5th June.

(*Mem.*: Curious, but authenticated fact, that a funeral is the only gathering to which the majority of men ever go willingly. Should like to think out why this should be so, but must instead unearth top-hat and other accoutrements of woe and try if open air will remove smell of naphthaline.)

June 7th. — Receive letter — (Why, in Heaven's name, not telegram?)—from Robert, to announce that godfather has left him Five Hundred Pounds. This strikes me as so utterly incredible and magnificent that I shed tears of pure relief and satisfaction. Mademoiselle comes in, in the midst of them, and on receiving explanation kisses me on both cheeks and exclaims: "Ah, je m'en doutais! Voilà bien ce bon Saint Antoine!" Can only draw conclusion that she has, most touchingly, been petitioning Heaven on our behalf, and very nearly weep again at the thought. Spend joyful evening making out lists of bills to be paid, jewellery to be redeemed, friends to be benefited, and purchases to be made, out of legacy, and am only slightly disconcerted on finding that net total of lists, when added together, comes to exactly one thousand three hundred and twenty pounds.

June 9th. — Return, yesterday, of Robert, and have every reason to believe that, though neither talkative nor exuberant, he fully appreciates newly achieved stability of financial position. He warmly concurs in my suggestion that great-aunt's diamond ring should be retrieved from Plymouth pawnbroker's in time to figure at our next excitement, which is the Garden Fête, and I accordingly hasten to Plymouth by earliest available bus.

Not only do I return with ring—(pawnbroker, after a glance at the calendar, congratulates me on being just in time)—but have also purchased new hat for myself, many yards of material for Vicky's frocks, a Hornby train for Robin, several gramophone records, and a small mauve bag for Mademoiselle. All give the utmost satisfaction, and I furthermore arrange to have hot lobster and fruit salad for dinner—these, however, not a great success with Robert, unfortunately, and he suggests—though kindly—that I was perhaps thinking more of my own tastes than of his, when devising this form of celebration. Must regretfully acknowledge truth in this. Discussion of godfather's legacy fills the evening happily, and I say that we ought to give a Party, and suggest combining it with Garden Fête. Robert replies, however,—and on further reflection find that I agree with him—that this would not conduce to the success of either entertainment, and scheme is abandoned. He also begs me to get Garden Fête over before I begin to think of anything else, and I agree to do so.

June 12*th.*—Nothing is spoken of but weather, at the moment propitious—but who can say whether similar conditions will prevail on 17th?—relative merits of having the Tea laid under the oak trees or near the tennis-court, outside price that can be reasonably asked for articles on Jumble Stall, desirability of having Ice-cream combined with Lemonade Stall, and the like. Date fortunately coincides with Robin's half-term, and I feel that he must and shall come home for the occasion. Expense, as I point out to Robert, now nothing to us. He yields. I become reckless, have thoughts of a House-party, and invite Rose to come down from London. She accepts.

Dear old school-friend Cissie Crabbe, by strange coincidence, writes that she will be on her way to Land's End on 16th June; may she stay for two nights? Yes, she may. Robert does not seem pleased when I explain that he will have to vacate his dressing-room for Cissie Crabbe, as Rose will be occupying spare bedroom, and Robin at home. This will complete House-party.

June 17th.—Entire household rises practically at dawn, in order to take part in active preparations for Garden Fête. Mademoiselle reported to have refused breakfast in order to put final stitches in embroidered pink satin boot-bag for Fancy Stall, which she has, to my certain knowledge, been working at for the past six weeks. At ten

o'clock our Vicar's wife dashes in to ask
what I think of the weather, and to say that
she cannot stop a moment. At eleven she is
still here, and has been joined by several stall-
holders, and tiresome local couple called
White, who want to know if there will be a
Tennis Tournament, and if not, is there not
still time to organise one? I reply curtly in
the negative to both suggestions and they
depart, looking huffed. Our Vicar's wife
says that this may have lost us their patron-
age at the Fête altogether, and that Mrs.
White's mother, who is staying with them,
is said to be rich, and might easily have been
worth a couple of pounds to us.

Diversion fortunately occasioned by unexpected arrival of solid and respectable-
looking claret-coloured motor-car, from
which Barbara and Crosbie Carruthers
emerge. Barbara is excited; C. C. remains
calm but looks benevolent. Our Vicar's
wife screams, and throws a pair of scissors
wildly into the air. (They are eventually
found in Bran Tub containing Twopenny

Dips, and are the cause of much trouble, as small child who fishes them out maintains them to be *bona fide* dip and refuses to give them up.)

Barbara looks blooming, and says how wonderful it is to see the dear old place quite unchanged. Cannot whole-heartedly agree with this, as it is not three months since she was here last, but fortunately she requires no answer, and says that she and C. C. are looking up old friends and will return for the Opening of the Fête this afternoon.

Robert goes to meet old school-friend Cissie Crabbe at station, and Rose and I to help price garments at Jumble Stall. (Find that my views are not always similar to those of other members of Committee. Why, for instance, only three-and-sixpence for grey georgette only sacrificed reluctantly at eleventh hour from my wardrobe?)

Arrival of Cissie Crabbe (wearing curious wool hat which I at once feel would look better on Jumble Stall) is followed by

cold lunch. Have made special point of re-
membering nuts and banana sandwiches for
Cissie, but have difficulty in preventing
Robin and Vicky—to whom I have omitted
to give explanation—making it obvious
that they would prefer this diet to cold
lamb and salad. Just as tinned pineapple
and junket stage is passed, Robin informs
me that there are people beginning to arrive,
and we all disperse in desperate haste and
excitement, to reappear in best clothes. I
wear red foulard and new red hat, but find
—as usual—that every petticoat I have in
the world is either rather too long or much
too short. Mademoiselle comes to the rescue
and puts safety-pins in shoulder-straps, one
of which becomes unfastened later and
causes me great suffering. Rose, also as
usual, looks nicer than anybody else in delightful green delaine. Cissie Crabbe also
has reasonably attractive dress, but detracts
from effect with numerous scarab rings,
cameo brooches, tulle scarves, enamel
buckles, and barbaric necklaces. Moreover,

she clings (I think mistakenly) to little wool hat, which looks odd. Robin and Vicky both present enchanting appearance, although Mary's three little Kellways, all alike in pale rose tussore, undeniably decorative. (Natural wave in hair of all three, which seems to me unjust, but nothing can be done until Vicky reaches age suitable for Permanent Waving.)

Lady Frobisher arrives—ten minutes too early—to open Fête, and is walked about by Robert until our Vicar says, Well, he thinks perhaps that we are now all gathered together. . . . (Have profane impulse to add "*In the sight of God*", but naturally stifle it.) Lady F. is poised gracefully on little bank under the chestnut tree, our Vicar beside her, Robert and myself modestly retiring a few paces behind, our Vicar's wife kindly, but mistakenly, trying to induce various unsuitable people to mount bank—which she humorously refers to as the Platform—when all is thrown into confusion by sensational arrival of colossal

LADY FROBISHER.

AW.

THE GARDENER.

Bentley containing Lady B.—in sapphire-blue and pearls—with escort of fashionable creatures, male and female, apparently dressed for Ascot.

"Go on, go on!" says Lady B., waving hand in white kid glove, and dropping small jewelled bag, lace parasol, and embroidered handkerchief as she does so. Great confusion while these articles are picked up and restored, but at last we do go on, and Lady F. says what a pleasure it is to her to be here to-day, what a desirable asset a Village Hall is, and much else to the same effect. Our Vicar thanks her for coming here to-day—so many claims upon her time—Robert seconds him with almost incredible brevity—someone else thanks Robert and myself for throwing open these magnificent grounds—(tennis-court, three flower borders, and microscopic shrubbery) —I look at Robert, who shakes his head, thus obliging me to make necessary reply myself, and our Vicar's wife, with undeniable presence of mind, darts forward and reminds Lady F. that she has forgotten to declare the Fête open. This is at once done, and we disperse to stalls and side-shows.

Am stopped by Lady B., who asks reproachfully, Didn't I know that she would have been perfectly ready to open the Fête herself, if I had asked her? Another time, she says, I am not to hesitate for a *moment*. She then spends ninepence on a lavender bag, and drives off again with expensive-looking friends. This behaviour provides topic of excited conversation for us all, throughout the whole of the afternoon.

Everyone else buys nobly, unsuitable articles are raffled—(raffling illegal, winner to pay sixpence)—guesses are made as to contents of sealed boxes, number of currants in large cake, weight of bilious-looking ham, and so on. Band arrives, is established on lawn, and plays selections from *The Geisha*. Mademoiselle's boot-bag bought by elegant purchaser in grey flannels, who turns out, on closer inspection, to

be Howard Fitzsimmons. Just as I recover
from this, Robin, in wild excitement, informs me that he has won a Goat in a raffle.
(Goat has fearful local reputation, and is of
immense age and savageness.) Have no time
to do more than say how *nice* this is, and he
had better run and tell Daddy, before old
Mrs. B., Barbara, C. C., and Cousin Maud
all turn up together. (Can baby Austin *possibly* have accommodated them all?) Old
Mrs. B. rather less subdued than at our last
meeting, and goes so far as to say that she
has very little money to spend, but that she
always thinks a smile and a kind word are
better than gold, with which I inwardly dis-
agree.

Am definitely glad to perceive that C. C.
has taken up cast-iron attitude of unfriend-
liness towards Cousin Maud, and contradicts her whenever she speaks. Sports, tea,
and dancing on the tennis-lawn all successful—(except possibly from point of view of
future tennis-parties)—and even Robin
and Vicky do not dream of eating final ice-

cream cornets, and retiring to bed, until ten o'clock.

Robert, Rose, Cissie Crabbe, Helen Wills, and myself all sit in the drawing-room in pleasant state of exhaustion, and congratulate ourselves and one another. Robert has information, no doubt reliable, but source remains mysterious, to the effect that we have Cleared Three Figures. All, for the moment, is *couleur-de-rose*.

June 23rd.—Tennis-party at wealthy and elaborate house, to which Robert and I now bidden for the first time. (Also, probably, the last.) Immense opulence of host and hostess at once discernible in fabulous display of deck-chairs, all of complete stability and miraculous cleanliness. Am introduced to youngish lady in yellow, and serious young man with horn-rimmed spectacles. Lady in yellow says at once that she is sure I have a lovely garden. (Why?)

Elderly, but efficient-looking, partner is assigned to me, and we play against the horn-rimmed spectacles and agile young creature in expensive crêpe-de-chine. Realise at once that all three play very much better tennis than I do. Still worse, realise that *they* realise this. Just as we begin, my partner observes gravely that he ought to tell me he is a left-handed player. Cannot imagine what he expects me to do about it, lose my head, and reply madly that That is Splendid.

Game proceeds, I serve several double-faults, and elderly partner becomes graver and graver. At beginning of each game he looks at me and repeats score with fearful distinctness, which, as it is never in our favour, entirely unnerves me. At "Six-*one*" we leave the court and silently seek chairs as far removed from one another as possible. Find myself in vicinity of Our Member, and we talk about the Mace, peeresses in the House of Lords—on which we differ— winter sports, and Alsatian dogs.

Robert plays tennis, and does well.

Later on, am again bidden to the court

and, to my unspeakable horror, told to play once more with elderly and efficient partner. I apologise to him for this misfortune, and he enquires in return, with extreme pessimism: Fifty years from now, what will it matter if we *have* lost this game? Neighbouring lady—probably his wife?—looks agitated at this, and supplements it by incoherent assurances about its being a great pleasure, in any case. Am well aware that she is lying, but intention evidently very kind, for which I feel grateful. Play worse than ever, and am not unprepared for subsequent enquiry from hostess as to whether I think I have *really* quite got over the measles, as she has heard that it often takes a full year. I reply, humorously, that, so far as tennis goes, it will take far more than a full year. Perceive by expression of civil perplexity on face of hostess that she has entirely failed to grasp this rather subtle witticism, and wish that I hadn't made it. Am still thinking about this failure, when I notice that conversation has, mysteriously, switched on to the United States of America, about which we are all very emphatic. Americans, we say, undoubtedly *hospitable* —but what about the War Debt? What about Prohibition? What about Sinclair Lewis, Aimée MacPherson, and Co-education? By the time we have done with them, it transpires that none of us have ever been to America, but all hold definite views, which fortunately coincide with the views of everybody else.

(Query: Could not interesting little experiment be tried, by possessor of unusual amount of moral courage, in the shape of suddenly producing perfectly bran-new opinion: for example, to the effect that Americans have better manners than we have, or that their divorce laws are a great improvement upon our own? Should much like to see effect of these, or similar, psychological bombs, but should definitely wish Robert to be absent from the scene.)

Announcement of tea breaks off these intelligent speculations.

Am struck, as usual, by infinite superiority of other people's food to my own.

Conversation turns upon Lady B. and everyone says she is really very kind-hearted, and follows this up by anecdotes illustrating all her less attractive qualities. Youngish lady in yellow declares that she met Lady B. last week in London, face three inches thick in new sunburn-tan. Can quite believe it. Feel much more at home after this, and conscious of new bond of union cementing entire party. Sidelight thus thrown upon human nature regrettable, but not to be denied. Even tennis improves after this, entirely owing to my having told funny story relating to Lady B.'s singular behaviour in regard to local Jumble Sale, which meets with success. Serve fewer double-faults, but still cannot quite escape conviction that whoever plays with me invariably loses the set—which I cannot believe to be mere coincidence.

Suggest to Robert, on the way home, that I had better give up tennis altogether, to

which, after long silence—during which I
hope he is perhaps evolving short speech
that shall be at once complimentary and yet
convincing—he replies that he does not
know what I could take up instead. As I do
not know either, the subject is dropped, and
we return home in silence.

June 27th.—Cook says that unless I am
willing to let her have the Sweep, she cannot possibly be responsible for the stove. I
say that of course she can have the Sweep.
If not, Cook returns, totally disregarding
this, she really can't say what won't happen.
I reiterate my complete readiness to send
the Sweep a summons on the instant, and
Cook continues to look away from me and
to repeat that unless I *will* agree to having
the Sweep in, there's no knowing.

This dialogue—cannot say why—upsets
me for the remainder of the day.

June 30th.—The Sweep comes, and de-
vastates the entire day. Bath-water and

meals are alike cold, and soot appears quite irrelevantly in portions of the house totally removed from sphere of Sweep's activities. Am called upon in the middle of the day to produce twelve-and-sixpence in cash, which I cannot do. Appeal to everybody in the house, and find that nobody else can, either. Finally Cook announces that the Joint has just come and can oblige at the back door, if I don't mind its going down in the book. I do not, and the Sweep is accordingly paid and disappears on a motor-bicycle.

July 3rd.—Breakfast enlivened by letter from dear Rose written at, apparently, earthly paradise of blue sea and red rocks, on South Coast of France. She says that she is having complete rest, and enjoying congenial society of charming group of friends, and makes unprecedented suggestion that I should join her for a fortnight. I am moved to exclaim—perhaps rather thoughtlessly —that the most wonderful thing in the world must be to be a childless widow—but this is met by unsympathetic silence from Robert, which recalls me to myself, and impels me to say that that isn't in the *least* what I meant.

(*Mem.*: Should often be very, very sorry to explain exactly what it is that I *do* mean, and am in fact conscious of deliberately avoiding self-analysis on many occasions. Do not propose, however, to go into this now or at any other time.)

I tell Robert that if it wasn't for the expense, and not having any clothes, and the servants, and leaving Vicky, I should think seriously of Rose's suggestion. Why, I enquire rhetorically, should Lady B. have a monopoly of the South of France? Robert replies, Well—and pauses for such a long while that I get agitated, and have mentally gone through the Divorce Court with him, before he ends up by saying Well, again, and picking up the *Western Morning News.* Feel—but do not say—that this, as contribution to discussion, is inadequate. Am pre-

pared, however, to continue it single-
handed sooner than allow subject to drop altogether. Do so, but am interrupted first by
entrance of Helen Wills through the window—(Robert says, Dam' that cat, I shall
have it drowned, but only absent-mindedly)
—and then by spirit-lamp, which is discovered to be extinct, and to require new
wick. Robert strongly in favour of ringing
immediately, but I discourage this, and undertake to speak about it instead, and tie
knot in pocket-handkerchief. (Unfortunately overcharged memory fails later when
in kitchen, and find myself unable to recollect whether marmalade has run to sugar
through remaining too long in jar, or
merely porridge lumpier than usual—but
this a digression.)

I read Rose's letter all over again, and
feel that I have here opportunity of a lifetime. Suddenly hear myself exclaiming
passionately that Travel broadens the
Mind, and am immediately reminded of our
Vicar's wife, who frequently makes similar

remark before taking our Vicar to spend fortnight's holiday in North Wales.

Robert finally says Well, again—this time tone of voice slightly more lenient—and then asks if it is quite impossible for his bottle of Eno's to be left undisturbed on bathroom shelf?

I at once and severely condemn Mademoiselle as undoubted culprit, although guiltily aware that original suggestion probably emanated from myself. And what, I add, about the South of France? Robert looks astounded, and soon afterwards leaves the dining-room without having spoken.

I deal with my correspondence, omitting Rose's letter. Remainder boils down to rather uninspiring collection of Accounts Rendered, offensive little pamphlet that makes searching enquiry into the state of my gums, postcard from County Secretary of Women's Institutes with notice of meeting that I am expected to attend, and warmly worded personal communication addressed me by name from unknown

Titled Gentleman, which ends up with a request for five shillings if I cannot spare more, in aid of charity in which he is interested. Whole question of South of France is shelved until evening, when I seek Mademoiselle in schoolroom, after Vicky has gone to bed. Am horrified to see that supper, awaiting her on the table, consists of cheese, pickles, and slice of jam roly-poly, grouped on single plate—(Would not this suggest to the artistic mind a Still-life Study in Modern Art?)—flanked by colossal jug of cold water. Is this, I ask, what Mademoiselle *likes?* She assures me that it is and adds, austerely, that food is of no importance to her. She could go without anything for days and days, without noticing it. From her early childhood, she has always been the same.

(Query unavoidably suggests itself here: Does Mademoiselle really expect me to believe her, and if so, what can be her opinion of my mental capacity?)

We discuss Vicky: tendency to argumentativeness, I hint. "C'est un petit cœur d'or," returns Mademoiselle immediately. I agree, in modified terms, and Mademoiselle at once points out dear Vicky's undeniable obstinacy and self-will, and goes so far as to say: "Plus tard, ce sera un esprit fort . . . elle ira loin, cette petite."

I bring up the subject of the South of France. Mademoiselle more than sympathetic, assures me that I must, at all costs, go, adding—a little unnecessarily—that I have grown many, many years older in the last few months, and that to live as I do, without any distractions, only leads to madness in the end.

Feel that she could hardly have worded this more trenchantly, and am a good deal impressed.

(Query: Would Robert see the force of these representations, or not? Robert apt to take rather prejudiced view of all that is not purely English.)

Return to drawing-room and find Robert asleep behind the *Times*. Read Rose's letter all over again, and am moved to make list of clothes that I should require if I joined her, estimate of expenses—financial situation, though not scintillating, still considerably brighter than usual, owing to recent legacy —and even Notes, on back of envelope, of instructions to be given to Mademoiselle, Cook, and the tradespeople, before leaving.

July 6th.—Decide definitely on joining Rose at Ste. Agathe, and write and tell her so. Die now cast, and Rubicon crossed—or rather will be, on achieving further side of the Channel. Robert, on the whole, takes lenient view of entire project, and says he supposes that nothing else will satisfy me, and better not count on really hot weather promised by Rose but take good supply of woollen underwear. Mademoiselle is sympathetic, but theatrical, and exclaims: "C'est la Ste. Vierge qui a tout arrangé!" which sounds like a travel agency, and shocks me.

Go to Women's Institute Meeting and tell our Secretary that I am afraid I shall have to miss our next Committee Meeting. She immediately replies that the date can easily be altered. I protest, but am defeated by small calendar, which she at once produces, and begs me to select my own date, and says that It will be All the Same to the eleven other members of the Committee.

(Have occasional misgivings at recollection of rousing speeches made by various speakers from our National Federation, to the effect that all W.I. members enjoy equal responsibilities and equal privileges. . . . Can only hope that none of them will ever have occasion to enter more fully into the inner workings of our Monthly Committee Meetings.)

July 1*2th.*—Pay farewell calls, and receive much good advice. Our Vicar says that it is madness to drink water anywhere in France, unless previously boiled and filtered; our Vicar's wife shares Robert's distrust as to climate, and advises Jaeger next the skin, and also offers loan of small

travelling medicine-chest for emergencies.
Discussion follows as to whether Bisulphate
of Quinine is, or is not, dutiable article, and
is finally brought to inconclusive conclusion
by our Vicar's pronouncing definitely that,
in *any* case, Honesty is the Best Policy.

Old Mrs. Blenkinsop—whom I reluctantly visit whenever I get a letter from
Barbara saying how grateful she is for my
kindness—adopts quavering and enfeebled
manner, and hopes she may be here to welcome me home again on my return, but
implies that this is not really to be anticipated. I say Come, come, and begin well-
turned sentence as to Mrs. B.'s wonderful
vitality, when Cousin Maud bounces in, and
inspiration fails me on the spot. What Ho!
says Cousin Maud—(or at least, produces
the effect of having said it, though possibly
slang slightly more up-to-date than this—
but not much)—What is all this about our
cutting a dash on the Lido or somewhere,
and leaving our home to take care of itself?
Talk about the Emancipation of Females,

says Cousin Maud. Should like to reply that no one, except herself, ever *does* talk about it—but feel this might reasonably be construed as uncivil, and do not want to upset unfortunate old Mrs. B., whom I now regard as a victim pure and simple. Ignore Cousin Maud, and ask old Mrs. B. what books she would advise me to take. Amount of luggage strictly limited, both as to weight and size, but could manage two very long ones, if in pocket editions, and another to be carried in coat-pocket for journey.

Old Mrs. B.—probably still intent on thought of approaching dissolution—suddenly says that there is nothing like the Bible—suggestion which I feel might more properly have been left to our Vicar. Naturally, give her to understand that I agree, but do not commit myself further. Cousin Maud, in a positive way that annoys me, recommends No book At All, especially when crossing the sea. It is well known, she affirms, that any attempt to fix the eyes on printed page while ship is moving induces

sea-sickness quicker than anything else.
Better repeat poetry, or the multiplication-
table, as this serves to distract the mind.
Have no assurance that the multiplication-
table is at my command, but do not reveal
this to Cousin Maud.

Old Mrs. B., abandoning Scriptural attitude, now says, Give her Shakespeare.
Everything is to be found in Shakespeare.
Look at *King Lear*, she says. Cousin Maud
assents with customary energy—but should
be prepared to take considerable bet that
she has never read a word of *King Lear*
since it was—presumably—stuffed down
her throat at dear old Roedean, in intervals
of cricket and hockey.

We touch on literature in general—old
Mrs. B. observes that much that is published nowadays seems to her unnecessary,
and why so much Sex in everything?—
Cousin Maud says that books collect dust,
anyway, and whisks away inoffensive copy
of *Time and Tide* with which old Mrs. B. is
evidently solacing herself in intervals of be-

ing hustled in and out of baby Austin—and I take my leave. Am embraced by old Mrs. B. (who shows tendency to have one of her old-time Attacks, but is briskly headed off it by Cousin Maud) and slapped on the back by Cousin Maud in familiar and extremely offensive manner.

Walk home, and am overtaken by well-known blue Bentley, from which Lady B. waves elegantly, and commands chauffeur to stop. He does so, and Lady B. says, Get in, Get in, never mind muddy boots— which makes me feel like a plough-boy. Good works, she supposes, have been taking me plodding round the village as usual? The way I go on, day after day, is too marvellous. Reply with utmost distinctness that I am just on the point of starting for the South of France, where I am joining party of distinguished friends. (This not entirely untrue, since dear Rose has promised introduction to many interesting acquaintances, including Viscountess.)

Really, says Lady B. But why not go at

the right time of year? Or why not go all
the way by sea?—yachting too marvellous.
Or why not, again, make it Scotland, instead of France?

Do not reply to any of all this, and request to be put down at the corner. This
is done, and Lady B. waves directions to
chauffeur to drive on, but subsequently
stops him again, and leans out to say that
she can find out all about quite inexpensive
pensions for me if I like. I do *not* like, and we
part finally.

Find myself indulging in rather melo-
dramatic fantasy of Bentley crashing into
enormous motor-bus and being splintered
to atoms. Permit chauffeur to escape unharmed, but fate of Lady B. left uncertain,
owing to ineradicable impression of earliest
childhood to the effect that It is Wicked to
wish for the Death of Another. Do not consider, however, that severe injuries, with
possible disfigurement, come under this
law—but entire topic unprofitable, and had
better be dismissed.

July 14*th*.—Question of books to be taken abroad undecided till late hour last night. Robert says, Why take any? and Vicky proffers *Les Malheurs de Sophie*, which she puts into the very bottom of my suit-case, whence it is extracted with some difficulty by Mademoiselle later. Finally decide on *Little Dorrit* and *The Daisy Chain*, with *Jane Eyre* in coat-pocket. Should prefer to be the kind of person who is inseparable from volume of Keats, or even Jane Austen, but cannot compass this.

July 15*th*.—*Mem.*: Remind Robert before starting that Gladys's wages due on Saturday. Speak about having my room turned out. Speak about laundry. Speak to Mademoiselle about Vicky's teeth, glyco-thymoline, Helen Wills *not* on bed, and lining of tussore coat. Write butcher. Wash hair.

July 17*th*.—Robert sees me off by early train for London, after scrambled and agitating departure, exclusively concerned with frantic endeavours to induce suit-case to shut. This is at last accomplished, but leaves me with conviction that it will be at least equally difficult to induce it to open again. Vicky bids me cheerful, but affectionate, good-bye and then shatters me at eleventh hour by enquiring trustfully if I shall be home in time to read to her after tea? As entire extent of absence has already been explained to her in full, this enquiry merely senseless—but serves to unnerve me badly, especially as Mademoiselle ejaculates: "Ah! la pauvre chère mignonne!" into the blue.

(*Mem.*: The French very often carried away by emotionalism to wholly preposterous lengths.)

Cook, Gladys, and the gardener stand at hall-door and hope that I shall enjoy my holiday, and Cook adds a rider to the effect that It seems to be blowing up for a gale, and for her part, she has always had a Norror of death by drowning. On this, we drive away.

"SCHOOLMASTER AND HIS WIFE . . . TALK TO ONE ANOTHER
ACROSS ME."

ELDERLY FRENCH COUPLE WITH TALKATIVE FRIEND.

Arrive at station too early—as usual—and I fill in time by asking Robert if he will telegraph if anything happens to the children, as I could be back again in twenty-four hours. He only enquires in return whether I have my passport? Am perfectly aware that passport is in my small purple dressing-case, where I put it a week ago, and have looked at it two or three times every day ever since—last time just before leaving my room forty-five minutes ago. Am nevertheless mysteriously impelled to open hand-bag, take out key, unlock small purple dressing-case, and verify presence of passport all over again.

(Query: Is not behaviour of this kind well known in therapeutic circles as symptomatic of mental derangement? Vague but disquieting association here with singular behaviour of Dr. Johnson in London streets —but too painful to be pursued to a finish.)

Arrival of train, and I say good-bye to Robert, and madly enquire if he would rather I gave up going at all? He rightly ignores this altogether.

(Query: Would not extremely distressing situation arise if similar impulsive offer were one day to be accepted? This gives rise to unavoidable speculation in regard to sincerity of such offers, and here again, issue too painful to be frankly faced, and am obliged to shelve train of thought altogether.)

Turn my attention to fellow-traveller— distrustful-looking woman with grey hair —who at once informs me that door of lavatory—opening out of compartment— has defective lock, and will *not* stay shut. I say Oh, in tone of sympathetic concern, and shut door. It remains shut. We watch it anxiously, and it flies open again. Later on, fellow-traveller makes fresh attempt, with similar result. Much of the journey spent in this exercise. I observe thoughtfully that Hope springs eternal in the human breast, and fellow-traveller looks more distrustful than ever. She finally says in despairing tones that Really, it isn't what she calls very nice, and lapses into depressed silence. Door remains triumphantly open.

Drive from Waterloo to Victoria, take out passport in taxi in order to Have It Ready, then decide safer to put it back again in dressing-case, which I do. (Dr. Johnson recrudesces faintly, but is at once dismissed.) Observe with horror that trees in Grosvenor Gardens are swaying with extreme violence in stiff gale of wind.

Change English money into French at Victoria Station, where superior young gentleman in little kiosk refuses to let me have anything smaller than one-hundred-franc notes. I ask what use *that* will be when it comes to porters, but superior young gentleman remains adamant. Infinitely competent person in blue and gold, labelled Dean & Dawson, comes to my rescue, miraculously provides me with change, says Have I booked a seat, pilots me to it, and tells me that he represents the best-known Travel Agency in London. I assure him warmly that I shall never patronise any other—which is true—and we part with mutual esteem. I make note on half of torn luggage-label to the effect that it would be merest honesty to write and congratulate D. & D. on admirable employé—but feel that I shall probably never do it.

Journey to Folkestone entirely occupied in looking out of train window and seeing quite large trees bowed to earth by force of wind. Cook's words recur most unpleasantly. Also recall various forms of advice received, and find it difficult to decide between going instantly to the Ladies' Saloon, taking off my hat, and lying down Perfectly Flat — (Mademoiselle's suggestion) — or Keeping in the Fresh Air at All Costs and Thinking about Other Things—(course advocated on a postcard by Aunt Gertrude). Choice taken out of my hands by discovery that Ladies' Saloon is entirely filled, within five minutes of going on board, by other people, who have all taken off their hats and are lying down Perfectly Flat.

Return to deck, sit on suit-case, and decide to Think about Other Things. Schoolmaster and his wife, who are going to Boulogne for a holiday, talk to one another across me about University Extension Course, and appear to be superior to the elements. I take out *Jane Eyre* from coat-pocket—partly in faint hope of impressing them, and partly to distract my mind—but remember Cousin Maud, and am forced to conclusion that she may have been right. Perhaps advice equally correct in respect of repeating poetry? Can think of nothing whatever, except extraordinary damp chill which appears to be creeping over me. Schoolmaster suddenly says to me: "Quite all *right*, aren't you?" To which I reply, Oh yes, and he laughs in a bright and scholastic way, and talks about the Matterhorn. Although unaware of any conscious recollection of it, find myself inwardly repeating curious and ingenious example of alliterative verse, committed to memory in my schooldays. (*Note*: Can dimly understand why the dying revert to impressions of early infancy.)

Just as I get to:

> "Cossack Commanders cannonading come
> Dealing destruction's devastating doom—"

elements overcome me altogether. Have dim remembrance of hearing schoolmaster exclaim in authoritative tones to everybody within earshot: "Make way for this lady— she is *Ill*"—which injunction he repeats every time I am compelled to leave suitcase. Throughout intervals, I continue to grapple, more or less deliriously, with alliterative poem, and do not give up altogether until

> "Reason returns, religious rights redound"

is reached. This I consider creditable.

Attain Boulogne at last, discover reserved seat in train, am told by several officials whom I question that we do, or alternatively, do not, change when we reach Paris, give up the elucidation of the point for the moment, and demand—and obtain—

small glass of brandy, which restores me.

July 18th, at Ste. Agathe.—Vicissitudes of travel very strange, and am struck—as often—by enormous dissimilarity between journeys undertaken in real life, and as reported in fiction. Can remember very few novels in which train journey of any kind does not involve either (*a*) Hectic encounter with member of opposite sex, leading to tense emotional issue; (*b*) discovery of murdered body in hideously battered condition, under circumstances which utterly defy detection; (*c*) elopement between two people each of whom is married to somebody else, culminating in severe disillusionment, or lofty renunciation.

Nothing of all this enlivens my own peregrinations, but on the other hand, the night not without incident.

Second-class carriage full, and am not fortunate enough to obtain corner-seat. American young gentleman sits opposite, and elderly French couple, with talkative friend wearing blue béret, who trims his nails with a pocket-knife and tells us about the state of the wine-trade.

I have dusty and elderly mother in black on one side, and her two sons—names turn out to be Guguste and Dédé—on the other. (Dédé looks about fifteen, but wears socks, which I think a mistake, but must beware of insularity.)

Towards eleven o'clock we all subside into silence, except the blue béret, who is now launched on tennis-champions, and has much to say about all of them. American young gentleman looks uneasy at mention of any of his compatriots, but evidently does not understand enough French to follow blue béret's remarks—which is as well.

Just as we all—except indefatigable béret, now eating small sausage-rolls—drop one by one into slumber, train stops at station and fragments of altercation break out in corridor concerning admission, or otherwise, of someone evidently accompanied by large dog. This is opposed by masculine voice repeating steadily, at short intervals: "Un chien n'est pas une personne," and heavily backed by assenting chorus, repeating after him: "Mais non, un chien n'est pas une personne."

To this I fall asleep, but wake a long time afterwards, to sounds of appealing enquiry, floating in from corridor: "Mais voyons— N'est-ce pas qu'un chien n'est pas une personne?"

The point still unsettled when I sleep again, and in the morning no more is heard, and I speculate in vain as to whether owner of the *chien* remained with him on the station, or is having *tête-à-tête* journey with him in separate carriage altogether. Wash inadequately, in extremely dirty accommodation provided, after waiting some time in lengthy queue. Make distressing discovery that there is no way of obtaining breakfast until train halts at Avignon. Break this information later to American young gentleman, who falls into deep distress and says

that he does not know the French for grape-
fruit. Neither do I, but am able to inform
him decisively that he will not require it.

Train is late, and does not reach Avignon
till nearly ten. American young gentleman
has a severe panic, and assures me that if he
leaves the train it will start without him.
This happened once before at Davenport,
Iowa. In order to avoid similar calamity, on
this occasion, I offer to procure him a cup
of coffee and two rolls, and successfully do
so—but attend first to my own require-
ments. We all brighten after this, and
Guguste announces his intention of shaving.
His mother screams, and says, "Mais c'est
fou"—with which I privately agree—and
everybody else remonstrates with Guguste
(except Dédé, who is wrapped in gloom),
and points out that the train is rocking, and
he will cut himself. The blue béret goes so
far as to predict that he will decapitate himself, at which everybody screams.

Guguste remains adamant, and produces
shaving apparatus and a little mug, which is

given to Dédé to hold. We all sit round in
great suspense, and Guguste is supported
by one elbow by his mother, while he conducts operations to a conclusion which produces no perceptible change whatever in his
appearance.

After this excitement, we all suffer from
reaction, and sink into hot and dusty silence.
Scenery gets rocky and sandy, with heat-
haze shimmering over all, and occasional
glimpses of bright blue-and-green sea.

At intervals train stops, and ejects various
people. We lose the elderly French couple
—who leave a Thermos behind them and
have to be screamed at by Guguste from
the window—and then the blue béret, eloquent to the last, and turning round on the
platform to bow as train moves off again.
Guguste, Dédé, and the mother remain with
me to the end, as they are going on as far as
Antibes. American young gentleman gets
out when I do, but lose sight of him altogether in excitement of meeting Rose,
charming in yellow embroidered linen. She

says that she is glad to see me, and adds that I look a Rag—which is true, as I discover on reaching hotel and looking-glass—but kindly omits to add that I have smuts on my face, and that petticoat has mysteriously descended two and a half inches below my dress, imparting final touch of degradation to general appearance.

She recommends bath and bed, and I agree to both, but refuse proffered cup of tea, feeling this would be altogether too reminiscent of English countryside, and quite out of place. I ask, insanely, if letters from home are awaiting me—which, unless they were written before I left, they could not possibly be. Rose enquires after Robert and the children, and when I reply that I feel I ought not really to have come away without them, she again recommends bed. Feel that she is right, and go there.

July 23rd.—Cannot avoid contrasting deliriously rapid flight of time when on a holiday, with very much slower passage of

ROSE.

ROBIN.

days, and even hours, in other and more familiar surroundings.

(*Mem.*: This disposes once and for all of fallacy that days seem long when spent in complete idleness. They seem, on the contrary, very much longer when filled with ceaseless activities.)

Rose—always so gifted in discovering attractive and interesting friends—is established in circle of gifted—and in some cases actually celebrated—personalities. We all meet daily on rocks, and bathe in sea. Temperature and surroundings very, very different to those of English Channel or Atlantic Ocean, and consequently find myself emboldened to the extent of quite active swimming. Cannot, however, compete with Viscountess, who dives, or her friend, who has unique and very striking method of doing back-fall into the water. Am, indeed, led away by spirit of emulation into attempting dive on one solitary occasion, and am convinced that I have plumbed the depths of the Mediterranean—have doubts, in fact, of ever leaving it again—but on enquiring of extremely kind spectator—(famous Headmistress)—How I went In, she replies gently: About level with the Water, she thinks—and we say no more about it.

July 25th.—Vicky writes affectionately, but briefly—Mademoiselle at greater length, and quite illegibly, but evidently full of hopes that I am enjoying myself. Am touched, and send each a picture-postcard. Robin's letter, written from school, arrives later, and contains customary allusions to boys unknown to me, also information that he has asked two of them to come and stay with him in the holidays, and has accepted invitation to spend a week with another. Postscript adds straightforward enquiry, Have I bought any chocolate yet?

I do so forthwith.

July 26th.—Observe in the glass that I look ten years younger than on arrival here, and am gratified. This, moreover, in spite of what I cannot help viewing as perilous adventure recently experienced in (temporarily) choppy sea, agitated by *vent d'est*, in which no one but Rose's Viscountess attempts to swim. She indicates immense and distant rock, and announces her intention of swimming to it. I say that I will go too. Long before we are half-way there, I know that I shall never reach it, and hope that Robert's second wife will be kind to the children. Viscountess, swimming calmly, says, Am I all right? I reply, Oh quite, and am immediately submerged.

(Query: Is this a Judgement?)

Continue to swim. Rock moves further and further away. I reflect that there will be something distinguished about the headlines announcing my demise in such exalted company, and mentally frame one or two that I think would look well in local paper. Am just turning my attention to paragraph in our Parish Magazine when I hit a small rock, and am immediately submerged again. Mysteriously rise again from the foam—though not in the least, as I know too well, like Venus.

Death by drowning said to be preceded by mental panorama of entire past life. Distressing reflection which very nearly causes me to sink again. Even *one* recollection from my past, if injudiciously selected, disconcerts me in the extreme, and cannot at all contemplate entire series. Suddenly perceive that space between myself and rock has actually diminished. Viscountess—who has kept near me and worn slightly anxious expression throughout—achieves it safely, and presently find myself grasping at sharp projections with tips of my fingers and bleeding profusely at the knees. Perceive that I have been, as they say, Spared.

(*Mem.*: Must try and discover for what purpose, if any.)

Am determined to take this colossal achievement as a matter of course, and merely make literary reference to Byron swimming the Hellespont—which would sound better if said in less of a hurry, and when not obliged to gasp, and spit out several gallons of water.

Minor, but nerve-racking, little problem here suggests itself: What substitute for a pocket-handkerchief exists when sea-bathing? Can conceive of no occasion—except possibly funeral of nearest and dearest—when this homely little article more frequently and urgently required. Answer, when it comes, anything but satisfactory.

I say that I am cold—which is true—and shall go back across the rocks. Viscountess, with remarkable tact, does not attempt to dissuade me, and I go.

July 27th.—End of holiday quite definitely in sight, and everyone very kindly says, Why not stay on? I refer, in return, to Robert and the children—and add, though not aloud, the servants, the laundry, the Women's Institute, repainting the outside of bath, and the state of my overdraft. Everyone expresses civil regret at my departure, and I go so far as to declare recklessly that I shall be coming back next year —which I well know to be unlikely in the extreme.

Spend last evening sending picture-post-cards to everyone to whom I have been intending to send them ever since I started.

July 29th, London.—Return journey accomplished under greatly improved conditions, travelling first-class in company with one of Rose's most distinguished friends. (Should much like to run across Lady B. by chance in Paris or elsewhere, but no such gratifying coincidence supervenes. Shall take care, however, to let her know circles in which I have been moving.)

Crossing as tempestuous as ever, and again have recourse to "An Austrian Army" with same lack of success as before. Boat late, train even more so, last available train for west of England has left Paddington long before I reach Victoria, and am obliged to stay night in London. Put through long-distance call to tell Robert this, but line is, as usual, in a bad way, and all I can hear is "What?" As Robert, on his side, can apparently hear even less, we do not get far. I find that I have no money, in spite of having borrowed from Rose—expenditure, as invariably happens, has exceeded estimate—but confide all to Secretary of my club, who agrees to trust me, but adds, rather disconcertingly—"as it's for one night only".

July 30*th.* — Readjustment sometimes rather difficult, after absence of unusual length and character.

July 31*st.*—The beginning of the holidays signalled, as usual, by the making of appointments with dentist and doctor. Photographs taken at Ste. Agathe arrive, and I am—perhaps naturally—much more interested in them than anybody else appears to be. (Bathing dress shows up as being even more becoming than I thought it was, though hair, on the other hand, not

at its best—probably owing to salt water.)
Notice, regretfully, how much more time I
spend in studying views of myself, than on
admirable group of delightful friends, or
even beauties of Nature, as exemplified in
camera studies of sea and sky.

Presents for Vicky, Mademoiselle, and
our Vicar's wife all meet with acclamation,
and am gratified. Blue flowered chintz frock,
however, bought at Ste. Agathe for sixty-
three francs, no longer becoming to me, as
sunburn fades and original sallowness returns to view. Even Mademoiselle, usually
so sympathetic in regard to clothes, eyes
chintz frock doubtfully, and says, "Tiens!
On dirait un bal masqué." As she knows,
and I know, that the neighbourhood never
has, and never will, run to *bals masqués*, this
equals unqualified condemnation of blue
chintz, and I remove it in silence to furthest
corner of the wardrobe.

Helen Wills, says Cook, about to produce more kittens. Cannot say if Robert
does, or does not, know this.

Spend much time in writing to, and hearing from, unknown mothers whose sons have been invited here by Robin, and one grandmother, with whose descendant Robin is to spend a week. Curious impossibility of combining dates and trains convenient to us all, renders this whole question harassing in the extreme. Grandmother, especially, sends unlimited letters and telegrams, to all of which I feel bound to reply—mostly with civil assurances of gratitude for her kindness in having Robin to stay. Very, very difficult to think of new ways of wording this—moreover, must reserve something for letter I shall have to write when visit is safely over.

August 1st.—Return of Robin, who has grown, and looks pale. He has also purchased large bottle of brilliantine, and applied it to his hair, which smells like inferior chemist's shop. Do not like to be unsympathetic about this, so merely remain silent while Vicky exclaims rapturously that it is *lovely*—which is also Robin's own opinion. They get excited and scream, and I suggest the garden. Robin says that he is hungry, having had no lunch. Practically— he adds conscientiously. "Practically" turns out to be packet of sandwiches, two bottles of atrocious liquid called Cherry Ciderette, slab of milk chocolate, two bananas purchased on journey, and small sample tin of cheese biscuits, swopped by boy called Sherlock, for Robin's last year's copy of *Pop's Annual.*

Customary rather touching display of affection between Robin and Vicky much to the fore, and am sorry to feel that repeated experience of holidays has taught me not to count for one moment upon its lasting more than twenty-four hours—if that.

(Query: Does motherhood lead to cynicism? This contrary to every convention of art, literature, or morality, but cannot altogether escape conviction that answer may be in the affirmative.)

In spite of this, however, cannot remain quite unmoved on hearing Vicky inform Cook that when she marries, her husband will be *exactly* like Robin. Cook replies indulgently, That's right, but come out of that sauce-boat, there's a good girl, and what about Master Robin's wife? To which Robin rejoins, he doesn't suppose he'll be *able* to get a wife exactly like Vicky, as she's so good, there couldn't be another one.

August 2nd.—Noteworthy what astonishing difference made in entire household by presence of one additional child. Robert finds one marble—which he unfortunately steps upon—mysterious little empty box with hole in bottom, and half of torn sponge on the stairs, and says, This house is a perfect Shambles—which I think excessive. Mademoiselle refers to sounds emitted by Robin, Vicky, the dog, and Helen Wills—all, apparently, gone mad together in the hay-loft—as "tohu-bohu". Very expressive word.

Meal-times, especially lunch, very, very far from peaceful. From time to time remember, with pained astonishment, theories subscribed to in pre-motherhood days, as to inadvisability of continually saying Don't, incessant fault-finding, and so on. Should now be sorry indeed to count number of times that I find myself forced to administer these and similar checks to the dear children. Am often reminded of enthusiastic accounts given me by Angela of other families, and admirable discipline obtaining there without effort on either side. Should like—or far more probably should *not* like —to hear what dear Angela says about *our* house, when visiting mutual friends or relations.

Rose writes cheerfully, still in South of France—sky still blue, rocks red, and bathing as perfect as ever. Experience curious illusion of receiving communication from another world, visited many aeons ago, and dimly remembered. Weather abominable, and customary difficulty experienced of finding indoor occupation for children that shall be varied, engrossing, and reasonably quiet. Cannot imagine what will happen if these conditions still prevail when visiting school-fellow—Henry by name—arrives. I ask Robin what his friend's tastes are, and he says, Oh, anything. I enquire if he likes cricket, and Robin replies, Yes, he expects so. Does he care for reading? Robin says that he does not know. I give it up, and write to Army and Navy Stores for large tin of Picnic Biscuits.

Messrs. R. Sydenham, and two unknown firms from places in Holland, send me little books relating to indoor bulbs. R. Sydenham particularly optimistic, and, though admitting that failures *have* been known, pointing out that all, without exception, have been owing to neglect of directions on page twenty-two. Immerse myself in page twenty-two, and see that there is nothing for it but to get R. Sydenham's Special Mixture for growing R. Sydenham's Special Bulbs.

Mention this to Robert, who does not encourage scheme in any way, and refers to last November. Cannot at the moment think of really good answer, but shall probably do so in church on Sunday, or in other surroundings equally inappropriate for delivering it.

August 3rd.—Difference of opinion arises between Robin and his father as to the nature and venue of former's evening meal, Robin making sweeping assertions to the effect that All Boys of his Age have Proper Late Dinner downstairs, and Robert replying curtly More Fools their Parents, which I privately think unsuitable language for use before children. Final and unsatisfactory compromise results in Robin's coming nightly to the dining-room and partaking of soup, followed by interval, and ending with dessert, during the whole of which Robert maintains disapproving silence and I talk to both at once on entirely different subjects.

(Life of a wife and mother sometimes very wearing.)

Moreover, Vicky offended at not being included in what she evidently looks upon as nightly banquet of Lucullan magnificence, and covertly supported in this rebellious attitude by Mademoiselle. Am quite struck by extraordinary persistence with which Vicky, day after day, enquires *Why* she can't stay up to dinner too? and equally phenomenal number of times that I reply with unvarying formula that Six years old is too young, darling.

Weather cold and disagreeable, and I complain. Robert asserts that it is really quite warm, only I don't take enough exercise. Have often noticed curious and prevalent masculine delusion, to the effect that sympathy should never, on any account, be offered when minor ills of life are in question.

Days punctuated by recurrent question as to whether grass is, or is not, too wet to be sat upon by children, and whether they shall, or shall not, wear their woollen pullovers. To all enquiries as to whether they are cold, they invariably reply, with aggrieved expressions, that they are *Boiling*. Should like scientific or psychological explanation of this singular state of affairs, and mentally reserve the question for bringing forward on next occasion of finding myself in intellectual society. This, however, seems at the moment remote in the extreme.

Cook says that unless help is provided in the kitchen they cannot possibly manage all the work. I think this unreasonable, and quite unnecessary expense. Am also aware that there is no help to be obtained at this time of the year. Am disgusted at hearing myself reply in hypocritically pleasant tone of voice that, Very well, I will see what can be done. Servants, in truth, make cowards of us all.

August 7th.—Local Flower Show takes place. We walk about in Burberrys, on wet grass, and say that it might have been much worse, and look at the day they had last week at West Warmington! Am forcibly reminded of what I have heard of Ruth Draper's admirable sketch of country Bazaar, but try hard not to think about this. Our Vicar's wife takes me to look at the school-children's needlework, laid out in tent amidst onions, begonias, and other vegetable products. Just as I am admiring pink cotton camisole embroidered with mauve pansies, strange boy approaches me and says, If I please, the little girl isn't very well, and can't be got out of the swing-boat, and will I come, please. I go, our Vicar's wife following, and saying—absurdly—that it must be the heat, and those swing-boats have always seemed to her very dangerous, ever since there was a fearful accident at her old home, when the whole thing broke down, and seven people were killed and a good many of the spectators injured. A relief, after this, to find Vicky merely green in the face, still clinging obstinately to the ropes and disregarding two men below saying Come along out of it, missie, and Now then, my dear, and Mademoiselle in terrific state of agitation, clasping her hands and pacing backwards and forwards, uttering many Gallic ejaculations and adjurations to the saints. Robin has removed himself to furthest corner of the ground, and is feigning interest in immense carthorse tied up in red ribbons.

(*N.B.* Dear Robin perhaps not so utterly unlike his father as one is sometimes tempted to suppose.)

I tell Vicky, very, very shortly, that unless she descends instantly, she will go to bed early every night for a week. Unfortunately, tremendous outburst of "Land of Hope and Glory" from brass band compels me to say this in undignified bellow, and to repeat it three times before it has any effect, by which time quite large crowd has gathered round. General outburst of applause when at last swing-boat is brought to a standstill, and Vicky—mottled to the last degree—is lifted out by man in check coat and tweed cap, who says *Here* we are, Amy Johnson! to fresh applause.

Vicky removed by Mademoiselle, not a moment too soon. Our Vicar's wife says that children are all alike, and it may be a touch of ptomaine poisoning, one never knows, and why not come and help her judge decorated perambulators?

Meet several acquaintances and newly-arrived Miss Pankerton, who has bought small house in village, and on whom I have not yet called. She wears pince-nez and is said to have been at Oxford. All I can get out of her is that the whole thing reminds her of Dostoeffsky.

Feel that I neither know nor care what she means. Am convinced, however, that I have not heard the last of either Miss P. or Dostoeffsky, as she assures me that she is the most unconventional person in the whole world, and never stands on ceremony. If she meets an affinity, she adds, she knows it directly, and then nothing can stop her. She just follows the impulse of the moment, and may as like as not stroll in for breakfast, or be strolled in upon for after-dinner coffee.

Am quite unable to contemplate Robert's reaction to Miss P. and Dostoeffsky at breakfast, and bring the conversation to an end as quickly as possible.

Find Robert, our Vicar, and neighbouring squire, looking at horses. Our Vicar and neighbouring squire talk about the weather, but do not say anything new. Robert says nothing.

Get home towards eight o'clock, strangely exhausted, and am discouraged at meeting both maids just on their way to the Flower-Show Dance. Cook says encouragingly that the potatoes are in the oven, and everything else on the table, and she only hopes Pussy hasn't found her way in, on account of the butter. Eventually do the washing-up, while Mademoiselle puts children to bed, and I afterwards go up and read *Tangle-wood Tales* aloud.

(Query, mainly rhetorical: Why are non-professional women, if married and with children, so frequently referred to as "leis-ured"? Answer comes there none.)

MISS PANKERTON.

JAHSPER.

August 8th.—Frightful afternoon, entirely filled by call from Miss Pankerton, wearing hand-woven blue jumper, wider in front than at the back, very short skirt, and wholly incredible small black béret. She smokes cigarettes in immense holder, and sits astride the arm of the sofa.

(*N.B.* Arm of the sofa not at all calculated to bear any such strain, and creaks several times most alarmingly. Must remember to see if anything can be done about it, and in any case manœuvre Miss P. into sitting elsewhere on subsequent visits, if any.)

Conversation very, very literary and academic, my own part in it being mostly confined to saying that I haven't yet read it, and, It's down on my library list, but hasn't come, so far. After what feels like some hours of this, Miss P. becomes personal, and says that I strike her as being a woman whose life has never known fulfilment. Have often thought exactly the same thing myself, but this does not prevent my feeling entirely furious with Miss P. for saying so. She either does not perceive, or is indifferent to, my fury, as she goes on to ask accusingly whether I realise that I have no *right* to let myself become a domestic beast of burden, with no interests beyond the nursery and the kitchen. What, for instance, she demands rousingly, have I read within the last two years? To this I reply weakly that I have read *Gentlemen Prefer Blondes*, which is the only thing I seem able to remember, when Robert and the tea enter simultaneously. Curious and difficult interlude follows, in the course of which Miss P. talks about the N.U.E.C.—(Cannot imagine what this is, but pretend to know all about it)—and the situation in India, and Robert either says nothing at all, or contradicts her very briefly and forcibly. Miss P. finally departs, saying that she is determined to scrape all the barnacles off me before she has done with me, and that I shall soon be seeing her again.

August 9th.—The child Henry deposited by expensive-looking parents in enormous red car, who dash away immediately, after one contemptuous look at house, garden, self, and children. (Can understand this, in a way, as they arrive sooner than expected, and Robin, Vicky, and I are all equally untidy owing to prolonged game of Wild Beasts in the garden.)

Henry unspeakably immaculate in grey flannel and red tie—but all is discarded when parents have departed, and he rapidly assumes disreputable appearance and loud, screeching tones of complete at-homeness. Robert, for reasons unknown, appears unable to remember his name, and calls him Francis. (Should like to trace connection of ideas, if any, but am baffled.)

Both boys come down to dinner, and Henry astonishes us by pouring out steady stream of information concerning speed-boats, aeroplanes, and submarines, from start to finish. Most informative. Am quite relieved, after boys have gone to bed, to find him looking infantile in blue-striped pyjamas, and asking to have door left open so that he can see light in passage outside.

I go down to Robert and ask—not very straightforwardly, since I know the answer only too well—if he would not like to take Mademoiselle, me, and the children to spend long day at the sea next week. We might invite one or two people to join us and have a picnic, say I with false optimism. Robert looks horrified and says, Surely that isn't necessary? but after some discussion, yields, on condition that weather is favourable.

(Should not be surprised to learn that he has been praying for rain ever since.)

August 1oth. — See Miss Pankerton through Post Office window and have serious thoughts of asking if I may just get under the counter for a moment, or retire into back premises altogether, but am restrained by presence of children, and also interesting story, embarked upon by Postmistress, concerning extraordinary decision of Bench, last Monday week, as to Separation Order applied for by Mrs. W. of the *Queen's Head*. Just as we get to its being well known that Mr. W. once threw hand-painted plate with view of Teignmouth right across the bedroom—absolutely right *across* it, from end to end, says Postmistress impressively—we are invaded by Miss P., accompanied by two sheep-dogs and some leggy little boys.

Little boys turn out to be nephews, paying a visit, and are told to go and make friends with Robin, Henry, and Vicky—at which all exchange looks of blackest hatred, with regrettable exception of Vicky, who smirks at the tallest nephew, who takes no notice. Miss P. pounces on Henry and says to me Is this my boy, his eyes are so exactly like mine she'd have known him anywhere. Nobody contradicts her, although I do not feel pleased, as Henry, in my opinion, entirely undistinguished-looking child.

Postmistress—perhaps diplomatically—

intervenes with, Did I say a two-shilling book, she has them, but I usually take the three-shilling, if I'll excuse her. I do excuse her, and explain that I only have two shillings with me, and she says that doesn't matter at all and Harold will take the other shilling when he calls for the letters. I agree to all, and turn cast-iron deafness to Miss P. in background exclaiming that this is Pure Hardy.

We all surge out of Post Office together, and youngest Pankerton nephew suddenly remarks that at *his* home the water once came through the bathroom floor into the dining-room. Vicky says Oh, and all then become silent again until Miss P. tells another nephew not to twist the sheep-dog's tail like that, and the nephew, looking astonished, says in return, Why not? to which Miss P. rejoins, Noel, that will *Do.*

Mem.: Amenities of conversation sometimes very curious, especially where society of children is involved. Have sometimes

wondered at what stage of development the
idea of continuity in talk begins to seem desirable—but here, again, disquieting reflection follows that perhaps this stage is never
reached at all. Debate for an instant
whether to put the point to Miss Pankerton,
but decide better not, and in any case, she
turns out to be talking about H. G. Wells,
and do not like to interrupt. Just as she is
telling me that it is quite absurd to compare
Wells with Shaw—(which I have never
thought of doing)—a Pankerton nephew
and Henry begin to kick one another on the
shins, and have to be told that that is Quite
Enough. The Pankerton nephew is agitated
and says, Tell him my name *isn't* Noah, it's
Noel. This misunderstanding cleared up,
but the nephew remains Noah to his con-
temporaries, and is evidently destined to do
so for years to come, and Henry receives
much applause as originator of brilliant
witticism.

Do not feel that Miss P. views any of it as
being in the least amusing, and in order to

create a diversion, rush into an invitation to them all to join projected picnic to the sea next week.

(Query: Would it not be instructive to examine closely exact motives governing suggestions and invitations that bear outward appearance of spontaneity? Answer: Instructive undoubtedly, but probably in many cases painful, and—on second thoughts— shall embark on no such exercise.)

We part with Pankertons at the cross-roads, but not before Miss P. has accepted invitation to picnic, and added that her brother will be staying with her then, and a dear friend who Writes, and that she hopes that will not be too large a party. I say No, not at all, and feel that this settles the question of buying another half-dozen picnic plates and enamel mugs, and better throw in a new Thermos as well, otherwise not a hope of things going round. That, says Miss P., will be delightful, and shall they bring their own sandwiches?—at which I exclaim in horror, and she says Really? and I say

Really, with equal emphasis but quite different inflection, and we part.

Robin says he does not know why I asked them to the picnic, and I stifle impulse to reply that neither do I, and Henry tells me all about hydraulic lifts.

Send children upstairs to wash for lunch, and call out several times that they must hurry up or they will be late, but am annoyed when gong, eventually, is sounded by Gladys nearly ten minutes after appointed hour. Cannot decide whether I shall, or shall not, speak about this, and am preoccupied all through roast lamb and mint sauce, but forget about it when fruit-salad is reached, as Cook has disastrously omitted banana and put in loganberries.

August 13*th.*—I tell Cook about the picnic lunch—for about ten people, say I—which sounds less than if I just said "ten" straight out—but she is not taken in by this, and at once declares that there isn't anything to make sandwiches of, that she can see, and butcher won't be calling till the day after to-morrow, and then it'll be scrag-end for Irish stew. I perceive that the moment has come for taking up absolutely firm stand with Cook, and surprise us both by suddenly saying Nonsense, she must order chicken from farm, and have it cold for sandwiches. It won't go round, Cook protests—but feebly— and I pursue advantage and advocate supplementary potted meat and hard-boiled eggs. Cook utterly vanquished, and I leave kitchen triumphant, but am met in the passage outside by Vicky, who asks in clarion tones (easily audible in kitchen and beyond) if I know that I threw cigarette-end into drawing-room grate, and that it has lit the fire all by itself?

August 15*th*.—Picnic takes place under singular and rather disastrous conditions, day not beginning well owing to Robin and Henry having strange overnight inspiration about sleeping out in summer-house, which is prepared for them with much elaboration

by Mademoiselle and myself — even to
crowning touch from Mademoiselle of small
vase of flowers on table. At 2 A.M. they decide that they wish to come in, and do so
through study window left open for them.
Henry involves himself in several blankets,
which he tries to carry upstairs, and trips
and falls down, and Robin knocks over hall-
stool, and treads on Helen Wills.

Robert and myself are roused, and Robert
is not pleased. Mademoiselle appears on
landing in *peignoir* and with head swathed
in little grey shawl, but screams at the sight
of Robert in pyjamas, and rushes away
again. (The French undoubtedly very curious mixture of modesty and the reverse.)

Henry and Robin show tendency to become explanatory, but are discouraged, and
put into beds. Just as I return down passage
to my room, sounds indicate that Vicky has
now awakened, and is automatically opening campaign by saying Can't I come
too? Instinct—unclassified, but evidently
stronger than maternal one—bids me leave

Mademoiselle to deal with this, which I un-hesitatingly do.

Get into bed again, feeling that the day has not opened very well, but sleep off and on until Gladys calls me—ten minutes late —but do not say anything about her un-punctuality, as Robert does not appear to have noticed it.

Sky is grey, but not necessarily threaten-ing, and glass has not fallen unreasonably. All is in readiness when Miss Pankerton (wearing Burberry, green knitted cap, and immense yellow gloves) appears in large Ford car which brims over with nephews, sheep-dogs, and a couple of men. Latter re-solve themselves into the Pankerton brother —who turns out to be from Vancouver— and the friend who Writes—very tall and pale, and is addressed by Miss P. in a pro-prietary manner as "Jahsper".

(Something tells me that Robert and Jahsper are not going to care about one another.)

After customary preliminaries about

weather, much time is spent in discussing arrangements in cars. All the children show tendency to wish to sit with their own relations rather than anybody else, except Henry, who says simply that the hired car looks much the best, and may he sit in front with the driver, please. All is greatly complicated by presence of the sheep-dogs, and Robert offers to shut them into an outhouse for the day, but Miss Pankerton replies that this would break their hearts, bless them, and they can just pop down anywhere amongst the baskets. (In actual fact, both eventually pop down on Mademoiselle's feet, and she looks despairing, and presently ask if I have by any chance a little bottle of eau-de-Cologne with me—which I naturally haven't.)

Picnic baskets, as usual, weigh incredible amount, and Thermos flasks stick up at inconvenient angles and run into our legs. (I quote "John Gilpin", rather aptly, but nobody pays any attention.)

When we have driven about ten miles,

rain begins, and goes on and on. Cars are stopped, and we find that two schools of thought exist, one—of which Miss P. is leader — declaring that we are Running out of It, and the other—headed by the Vancouver brother and heavily backed by Robert—that we are Running into It. Miss P.—as might have been expected—wins, and we proceed; but Run into It more and more. By the time destination is reached, we have Run into It to an extent that makes me wonder if we shall ever Run out of It.

Lunch has to be eaten in three bathing huts, hired by Robert, and the children become hilarious and fidgety. Miss P. talks about Companionate Marriage to Robert, who makes no answer, and Jahsper asks me what I think of James Elroy Flecker. As I cannot remember exact form of J. E. F.'s activities, I merely reply that in many ways he was very wonderful—which no doubt he was—and Jahsper seems satisfied, and eats tomato sandwiches. The children ask riddles —mostly very old and foolish ones—and

Miss P. looks annoyed, and says See if it has stopped raining—which it hasn't. I feel that she and the children must, at all costs, be kept apart, and tell Robert in urgent whisper that, rain or no rain, they must go out.

They do.

Miss Pankerton becomes expansive, and suddenly remarks to Jahsper that *Now* he can see what she meant, about positively Victorian survivals still to be found in English family life. At this, Vancouver brother looks aghast—as well he may—and dashes out into the wet. Jahsper says Yerse, Yerse, and sighs, and I at once institute vigorous search for missing plate, which creates a diversion.

Subsequently the children bathe, get wetter than ever, drip all over the place, and are dried—Mademoiselle predicts death from pneumonia for all—and we seek the cars once more. One sheep-dog is missing, but eventually recovered in soaking condition, and is gathered on to united laps of

Vicky, Henry, and a nephew. I lack energy to protest, and we drive away.

Beg Miss P., Jahsper, brother, nephews, sheep-dogs, and all, to come in and get dry and have tea, but they have the decency to refuse, and I make no further effort, but watch them depart with untold thankfulness.

(Should be sorry to think impulses of hospitality almost entirely dependent on convenience, but cannot altogether escape suspicion that this is so.)

Robert extremely forbearing on the whole, and says nothing worse than Well!—but this very expressively.

August 16*th*.—Robert, at breakfast, suddenly enquires if that nasty-looking fellow does anything for a living? Instinct at once tells me that he means Jahsper, but am unable to give him any information, except that Jahsper writes, which Robert does not appear to think is to his credit. He goes so far as to say that he hopes yesterday's rain may put an end to him altogether—but whether this means to his presence in the neighbourhood, or to his existence on this planet, am by no means certain, and prefer not to enquire. Ask Robert instead if he did not think, yesterday, about Miss Edgeworth, Rosamond, and the Party of Pleasure, but this wakens no response, and conversation—such as it is—descends once more to level of slight bitterness about the coffee, and utter inability to get really satisfactory bacon locally. This is only brought to a close by abrupt entrance of Robin, who remarks without preliminary: "Isn't Helen Wills going to have kittens almost at once? Cook thinks so."

Can only hope that Robin does not catch exact wording of short ejaculation with which his father receives this.

August 18*th.*—Pouring rain, and I agree to let all three children dress up, and give them handsome selection from my wardrobe for the purpose. This ensures me brief

half-hour uninterrupted at writing-table,
where I deal with baker—brown bread far
from satisfactory—Rose—on a picture-postcard of Backs at Cambridge, which mysteriously appears amongst stationery—Robin's
Headmaster's wife—mostly about stockings, but Boxing may be substituted for
Dancing, in future—and Lady Frobisher,
who would be so delighted if Robert and I
would come over for tea whilst there is still
something to be seen in the garden. (Do not
like to write back and say that I would far
rather come when there is nothing to be
seen in the garden, and we might enjoy excellent tea in peace—so, as usual, sacrifice
truth to demands of civilisation.)

Just as I decide to tackle large square envelope of thin blue paper, with curious
purple lining designed to defeat anyone en-
deavouring to read letter within—which
would anyhow be impossible, as Barbara
Carruthers always most illegible—front-
door bell rings.

Thoughts immediately fly to Lady B.,

and I rapidly rehearse references that I intend to make to recent stay in South of France—(shall not specify length of visit)—and cordial relations there established with distinguished society, and Rose's Viscountess in particular. Have also sufficient presence of mind to make use of pocket comb, mirror, and small powder-puff kept for emergencies in drawer of writing-table. (Discover, much later, that I have overdone powder-puff very considerably, and reflect, not for the first time, that we are spared much by inability—so misguidedly deplored by Scottish poet—to see ourselves as others see us.)

Door opens, and Miss Pankerton is shown in, followed—it seems to me reluctantly—by Jahsper. Miss P. has on military-looking cape, and béret as before, which strikes me as odd combination, and anyhow cape looks to me as though it might drip rain-drops on furniture, and I beg her to take it off. This she does with rather spacious gesture—(Can she have been seeing *The Three Musketeers* at local cinema?)—and unfortunately one end of it, apparently heavily weighted, hits Jahsper in the eye. Miss P. is very breezy and off-hand about this, but Jahsper, evidently in severe pain, falls into deep dejection, and continues to hold large yellow crêpe-de-chine handkerchief to injured eye for some time. Am distracted by wondering whether I ought to ask him if he would like to bathe it—which would involve taking him up to bathroom, probably untidy— and trying to listen intelligently to Miss P., who is talking about Proust.

This leads, by process that I do not follow, to a discussion on Christian names, and Miss P. says that All Flower Names are Absurd. Am horrified to hear myself replying, senselessly, that I think Rose is a pretty name, as one of my greatest friends is called Rose—to which Miss P. rightly answers that that, really, has nothing to do with it, and Jahsper, still dabbing at injured eye, contributes austere statement to the effect that only the Russians really understand Beauty in Nomenclature.

Am again horrified at hearing myself inter-
ject "*Ivan Ivanovitch*" in entirely detached
and irrelevant manner, and really begin to
wonder if mental weakness is overtaking me.
Moreover, am certain that I have given Miss
P. direct lead in the direction of Dostoeffsky, about whom I do not wish to hear, and
am altogether unable to converse.

Entire situation is, however, revolution-
ised by totally unexpected entrance of
Robin—staggering beneath my fur coat
and last summer's red crinoline straw hat—
Henry, draped in blue kimono, several
scarfs belonging to Mademoiselle, old pair
of fur gloves, with scarlet school-cap inap-
propriately crowning all—and Vicky, wearing nothing whatever but small pair of
green silk knickerbockers and large and
unfamiliar black felt hat put on at rakish
angle.

Completely stunned silence overtakes us
all, until Vicky, advancing with perfect
aplomb, graciously says, "How do you do?"
and shakes hands with Jahsper and Miss P.

in turn, and I succeed in surpassing already well-established record for utter futility, by remarking that They have been Dressing Up.

Atmosphere becomes very, very strained indeed, only Vicky embarking on sprightly reminiscences of recent picnic, which meet with no response. Final depths of unsuccess are plumbed, when it transpires that Vicky's black sombrero, picked up in the hall, is in reality the property of Jahsper. I apologise profusely, the children giggle, Miss P. raises her eyebrows to quite unnatural heights, and gets up and looks at the book-shelves in a remote and superior way, and Jahsper says, Oh, never mind, it really is of no consequence, at the same time receiving hat with profound solicitude, and dusting it with two fingers.

Greatest possible relief when Miss P. declares that they must go, otherwise they will miss the Brahms Concerto on the wireless. I hastily agree that this would never do, and tell Robin to open the door. Just as we all cross the hall, Gladys is inspired to sound the gong for tea, and I am compelled to say, Won't they stay and have some? but Miss P. says she never takes anything at all between lunch and dinner, thanks, and Jahsper pretends he hasn't heard me and makes no reply whatever.

They march out into pouring rain, Miss P. once more giving martial fling to military cape—(at which Jahsper flinches, and removes himself some yards away from her) —and entirely disdaining small and elegant umbrella beneath which Jahsper and his black felt take refuge. Robin enquires, in tones of marked distaste, if I *like* those people? but I feel it better to ignore this, and recommend getting washed for tea. Customary discussion follows as to whether washing is, or is not, necessary.

(*Mem.*: Have sometimes considered— though idly—writing letter to the *Times* to find out if any recorded instances exist of parents and children whose views on this subject coincide. Topic of far wider appeal than many of those so exhaustively dealt with.)

August 25th.—Am displeased by Messrs. R. Sydenham, who have besought me, in urgently worded little booklet, to Order Bulbs Early, and when I do so—at no little inconvenience, owing to customary pressure of holidays—reply on a postcard that order will be forwarded "when ready". Have serious thoughts of cancelling the whole thing—six selected, twelve paper-whites, à dozen early assorteds, and a half bushel of Fibre, Moss, and Charcoal. Cannot very well do this, however, owing to quite recent purchase of coloured bowls from Woolworth's, as being desirable additions to existing collection of odd pots, dented enamel basins, large red glass jam-dish, and dear grandmamma's disused willow-pattern foot-bath.

Departure of the boy Henry—who says that he has enjoyed himself, which I hope is true—accompanied by Robin, who is to be met and extracted from train at Salisbury by uncle of boy with whom he is to stay.

(Query: How is it that others are so frequently able to obtain services of this nature from their relations? Feel no conviction that either William or Angela · would react favourably, if called upon to meet unknown children at Salisbury or anywhere else.)

Vicky, Mademoiselle, and I wave goodbye from hall door—rain pouring down as usual—and Vicky seems a thought depressed at remaining behind. This tendency greatly enhanced by Mademoiselle's exclamation, on retiring into the house once more—"On dirait un tombeau!"

Second post brings letter from Barbara in the Himalayas, which gives me severe shock of realising that I haven't yet read her last one, owing to lack of time and general impression that it is illegibly scrawled and full of allusions to native servants. Remorsefully open this one, perceive with relief that it is quite short and contains nothing that looks like native servants, but very interesting piece of information, rather circuitously worded by dear Barbara, but still quite beyond misunderstanding. I tell Mademoiselle, who says "Ah, comme c'est touchant!" and at once wipes her eyes—display which I think excessive.

Robert, to whom I also impart news, goes to the other extreme, and makes no comment except "I daresay". On the other hand, our Vicar's wife calls, for the express purpose of asking whether I think it will be a boy or a girl, and of suggesting that we should at once go together and congratulate old Mrs. Blenkinsop. I remind her that Barbara stipulates in letter for secrecy, and our Vicar's wife says, Of course, of course—it had slipped her memory for the moment—but surely old Mrs. B. must know all about it? However, she concedes that dear Barbara may perhaps not wish her mother to know that we know, just yet, and concludes with involved quotation from Thomas à Kempis about exercise of discretion. We then discuss educational facilities in the Himalayas, the Carruthers nose—which neither of us cares about—and the desirability or otherwise of having twins. Our Vicar's wife refuses tea, talks about books—she likes to have something *solid* in hand, always—is reminded of Miss Pankerton, about whom she is doubtful, but admits that it is early days to judge—again refuses tea, and assures me that she must go. She eventually stays to tea, and walks up and down the lawn with me afterwards, telling me of Lady B.'s outrageous behaviour in connection with purchase of proposed site for the Village Hall. This, as usual, serves to unite us in warm friendship, and we part cordially.

August 28th.—Picnic, and Cook forgets to put in the sugar. Postcard from Robin's hostess says that he has arrived, but adds nothing as to his behaviour, or impression that he is making, which makes me feel anxious.

August 31*st.*—Read *The Edwardians*—which everybody else has read months ago—and am delighted and amused. Remember that V. Sackville-West and I once attended dancing classes together at the Albert Hall, many years ago, but feel that if I do mention this, everybody will think I am boasting—which indeed I should be—so better forget about it again, and in any case, dancing never my strongest point, and performance at Albert Hall extremely mediocre and may well be left in oblivion. Short letter from Robin which I am very glad to get, but which refers to nothing whatever except animals at home, and project for going out in a boat and diving from it on some unspecified future occasion. Reply to all, and am too modern to beg tiresomely for information concerning himself.

September 1*st.*—Postcard from the station announces arrival of parcel, that I at once identify as bulbs, with accompanying Fibre, Moss, and Charcoal mixture. Suggest that

Robert should fetch them this afternoon, but he is unenthusiastic, and says to-morrow, when he will be meeting Robin and school-friend, will do quite well.

(*Mem.*: Very marked difference between the sexes is male tendency to procrastinate doing practically everything in the world except sitting down to meals and going up to bed. Should like to purchase little painted motto: *Do it now*, so often on sale at inferior stationers' shops, and present it to Robert, but on second thoughts quite see that this would not conduce to domestic harmony, and abandon scheme at once.)

Think seriously about bulbs, and spread sheets of newspaper on attic floor to receive them and bowls. Resolve also to keep careful record of all operations, with eventual results, for future guidance. Look out notebook for the purpose, and find small green booklet, with mysterious references of which I can make neither head nor tail, in own handwriting on two first pages. Spend some time in trying to decide what I could have

T

meant by: Kp. p. in sh. twice p. w. *without fail* or: Tell H. *not* 12″ by 8″ Washable f.c. to be g'd, but eventually give it up, and tear out two first pages of little green book, and write BULBS and to-morrow's date in capital letters.

September 2nd.—Robert brings home Robin, and friend called Micky Thompson, from station, but has unfortunately forgotten to call for the bulbs. Micky Thompson is attractive and shows enchanting dimple whenever he smiles, which is often.

(*Mem.*: Theory that mothers think their own children superior to any others Absolute Nonsense. Can see only too plainly that Micky easily surpasses Robin and Vicky in looks, charm, and good manners—and am very much annoyed about it.)

September 4th.—Micky Thompson continues to show himself as charming child, with cheerful disposition, good manners, and excellent health. Enquiry reveals that he is an orphan, which does not surprise me in the least. Have often noticed that absence of parental solicitude usually very beneficial to offspring. Bulbs still at station.

September 10th.—Unbroken succession of picnics, bathing expeditions, and drives to Plymouth Café in search of ices. Mademoiselle continually predicts catastrophes to digestions, lungs, or even brains—but none materialise.

September 11th.—Departure of Micky Thompson, but am less concerned with this than with Robert's return from station, this time accompanied by bulbs and half-bushel of Fibre, Moss, and Charcoal. Devote entire afternoon to planting these, with much advice from Vicky and Robin, and enter full details of transaction in little green book. Prepare to carry all, with utmost care, into furthest and darkest recess of attic, when Vicky suddenly announces that Helen

Wills is there already, with six bran-new kittens.

Great excitement follows, which I am obliged to suggest had better be modified before Daddy enquires into its cause. Children agree to this, but feel very little confidence in their discretion. Am obliged to leave bulbs in secondary corner of attic, owing to humane scruples about disturbing H. Wills and family.

September 20*th*.—Letter from County Secretary of adjoining County, telling me that she knows how busy I am—which I'm certain she doesn't—but Women's Institutes of Chick, Little March, and Crimpington find themselves in terrible difficulty owing to uncertainty about next month's speaker. Involved fragments about son coming, or not coming, home on leave from Patagonia, and daughter ill—but not dangerously—at Bromley, Kent—follow. President is away —(further fragment, about President being obliged to visit aged relative while aged relative's maid is on holiday)—and County Secretary does not know what to do. What she does do, however, is to suggest that I should be prepared to come and speak at all three Institute meetings, if—as she rather strangely puts it—the worst comes to the worst. Separate half-sheet of paper gives details about dates, times, and bus between Chick and Little March, leading on to doctor's sister's two-seater, at cross-roads between Little March and Crimpington Hill. At Crimpington, County Secretary concludes triumphantly, I shall be put up for the night by Lady Magdalen Crimp— always so kind, and such a friend to the Movement — at Crimpington Hall. *P.S.* Travel talks always popular, but anything I like will be delightful. Chick very keen about Folk Lore, Little March more on the Handicraft side. *But anything I like. P.P.S.* Would I be so kind as to judge Recitation Competition at Crimpington?

I think this over for some time, and decide to write and say that I will do it, as

Robin will have returned to school next week, and should like to distract my mind. Tell Mademoiselle casually that I may be going on a short tour, speaking, and she is suitably impressed. Vicky enquires: "Like a menagerie, mummie?" which seems to me very extraordinary simile, though innocently meant. I reply, "No, not in the least like a menagerie," and Mademoiselle adds, officiously, "More like a mission." Am by no means at one with her here, but have no time to go further into the subject, as Gladys summons me to prolonged discussion with the Laundry—represented by man in white coat at the back gate—concerning cotton sheet, said to be one of a pair, but which has been returned in solitary widowhood. The Laundry has much to say about this, and presently Cook, gardener, Mademoiselle, Vicky, and unidentified boy apparently attached to Laundry, have all gathered round. Everyone except boy supports Gladys by saying "That's right" to everything she asserts, and I eventually leave them to it. Evidently all takes time, as it is not till forty minutes later that I see gardener slowly returning to his work, and hear van driving away.

Go up to attic and inspect bulb-bowls, but nothing to be seen. Cannot decide whether they require water or not, but think perhaps better be on the safe side, so give them some. Make note in little green book to this effect, as am determined to keep full record of entire procedure.

September 22nd.—Invitation from Lady B.—note delivered by hand, wait reply—to Robert and myself to come and dine tonight. Reads more like a Royal Command, and no suggestion that short notice may be inconvenient. Robert out, and I act with promptitude and firmness on own responsibility, and reply that we are already engaged for dinner.

(Query: Will this suggest convivial evening at neighbouring Rectory, or rissoles and cocoa with old Mrs. Blenkinsop and Cousin

Maud? Can conceive of no other alternatives.)

Telephone rings in a peremptory manner just as I am reading aloud enchanting book, *The Exciting Family* by M. D. Hillyard— (surely occasional contributor to *Time and Tide?*)—and I rush to dining-room to deal with it. (*N.B.* Must really overcome foolish and immature tendency to feel that any telephone-call may be prelude to (*a*) announcement of a fortune or, alternatively, (*b*) news of immense and impressive calamity.)

On snatching up receiver, unmistakable tones of Lady B. are heard—at once suggesting perhaps rather ill-natured, but not unjustifiable, comparison with a pea-hen. What, she enquires, is all this nonsense? Of course we must dine to-night—she won't hear of a refusal. Besides, what else can we possibly be doing, unless it's Meetings, and if so, we can cut them for once.

Am at once invaded by host of improbable inspirations: *e.g.* that the Lord-Lieutenant of the County and his wife are dining here informally, or that Rose's Viscountess is staying with us and refuses either to be left alone or to be taken to Lady B.'s—(which I know she would at once suggest)—or even that, really, Robert and I have had so many late nights recently that we cannot face another one—but do not go so far as to proffer any of them aloud. Am disgusted, instead, to hear myself saying weakly that Robin goes back to school day after to-morrow, and we do not like to go out on one of his last few evenings at home. (This may be true so far as I am concerned, but can imagine no suggestion less likely to be endorsed by Robert, and trust that he may never come to hear of it.) In any case, it instantly revives long-standing determination of Lady B.'s to establish me with reputation for being a Perfect Mother, and she at once takes advantage of it.

I return to *The Exciting Family* in a state of great inward fury.

September 24th. — Frightful welter of packing, putting away, and earnest consultations of School List. Robin gives everybody serious injunctions about not touching anything *whatever* in his bedroom—which looks like inferior pawnbroking establishment at stocktaking time—and we all more or less commit ourselves to leaving it alone till Christmas holidays—which is completely out of the question.

He is taken away by Robert in the car, looking forlorn and infantile, and Vicky roars. I beseech her to desist at once, but am rebuked by Mademoiselle, who says, "Ah, elle a tant de cœur!" in tone which implies that she cannot say as much for myself.

October 1st.—Tell Robert about proposed short tour to Chick, Little March, and Crimpington, on behalf of W.Is. He says little, but that little not very enthusiastic. I spend many hours—or so it seems —looking out Notes for Talks, and trying to remember anecdotes that shall be at once funny and suitable. (This combination rather unusual.)

Pack small bag, search frantically all over writing-table, bedroom, and drawing-room for W.I. Badge—which is at last discovered by Mademoiselle in remote corner of drawer devoted to stockings—and take my departure. Robert drives me to station, and I beg that he will keep an eye on the bulbs whilst I am away.

October 2nd.—Bus from Chick conveys me to Little March, after successful meeting last night, at which I discourse on Amateur Theatricals, am applauded, thanked by President in the chair—name inaudible—applauded once more, and taken home by Assistant Secretary, who is putting me up for the night. We talk about the Movement —Annual Meeting at Blackpool perhaps a mistake, why not Bristol or Plymouth?—difficulty of thinking out new Programmes for monthly meetings, and really magnificent performance of Chick at recent Folk-dancing Rally, at which Institute members called upon to go through "Gathering Peascods" no less than three times—two of Chick's best performers, says Assistant Secretary proudly, being grandmothers. I express astonished admiration, and we go on to Village Halls, Sir Oswald Mosley, and methods of removing ink-stains from linen. Just as Assistant Secretary—who is unmarried and lives in nice little cottage—has escorted me to charming little bedroom, she remembers that I am eventually going on to Crimpington, and embarks on interesting scandal about two members of Institute there, and unaccountable disappearance of one member's name from Committee. This keeps us up till eleven o'clock, when she begs me to say nothing whatever about her having mentioned the affair, which was all told her in strictest confidence, and we part.

Reach Little March, via the bus—which is old, and rattles—in time for lunch. Doctor's sister meets me—elderly lady with dog—and talks about hunting. Meeting takes place at three o'clock, in delightful Hut, and am impressed by business-like and efficient atmosphere. Doctor's sister, in the chair, introduces me—unluckily my name eludes her at eleventh hour, but I hastily supply it and she says, "Of course, of course" —and I launch out into A Visit to Switzerland. As soon as I have finished, elderly member surges up from front row and says that this has been particularly interesting to *her*, as she once lived in Switzerland for nearly fourteen years and knows every inch of it from end to end. (My own experience confined to six weeks round and about Lucerne, ten years ago.)

We drink cups of tea, eat excellent buns, sing several Community Songs, and Meeting comes to an end. Doctor's sister's two-seater, now altogether home-like, receives me once again, and I congratulate her on Institute. She smiles and talks about hunting.

Evening passes off quietly, doctor comes

in—elderly man with two dogs—he also talks about hunting, and we all separate for bed at ten o'clock.

October 3rd.—Part early from doctor, sister, dogs, and two-seater, and proceed by train to Crimpington, as Meeting does not take place till afternoon, and have no wish to arrive earlier than I need. Curious cross-country journey with many stops, and one change involving long and draughty wait that I enliven by cup of Bovril.

Superb car meets me, with superb chauffeur who despises me and my bag at sight, but is obliged to drive us both to Crimpington Hall. Butler receives me, and I am conducted through immense and chilly hall with stone flags to equally immense and chilly drawing-room, where he leaves me. Very small fire is lurking behind steel bars at far end of room, and I make my way to it past little gilt tables, large chairs, and sofas, cabinets apparently lined with china cups and lustre tea-pots, and massive writing-

tables entirely furnished with hundreds of
photographs in silver frames. Butler suddenly reappears with the *Times*, which he
hands to me on small salver. Have already
read it from end to end in the train, but feel
obliged to open it and begin all over again.
He looks doubtfully at the fire, and I hope
he is going to put on more coal, but instead
he goes away, and is presently replaced by
Lady Magdalen Crimp, who is about
ninety-five and stone-deaf. She wears black,
and large fur cape—as well she may. She
produces trumpet, and I talk down it, and
she smiles and nods, and has evidently not
heard one word—which is just as well, as
none of them worth hearing. After some
time she suggests my room, and we creep
along slowly for about quarter of a mile,
till first floor is reached, and vast bedroom
with old-fashioned four-poster in the middle
of it. Here she leaves me, and I wash, from
little brass jug of tepid water, and note—by
no means for the first time—that the use of
powder, when temperature has sunk below

a certain level, merely casts extraordinary azure shade over nose and chin.

Faint hope of finding fire in dining-room is extinguished on entering it, when I am at once struck by its resemblance to a mausoleum. Lady M. and I sit down at mahogany circular table, she says Do I mind a Cold Lunch? I shake my head, as being preferable to screaming "No" down trumpet—though equally far from the truth—and we eat rabbit-cream, coffee-shape, and Marie biscuits.

Conversation spasmodic and unsatisfactory, and I am reduced to looking at portraits on wall, of gentlemen in wigs and ladies with bosoms, also objectionable study of dead bird, dripping blood, lying amongst oranges and other vegetable matter. (Should like to know what dear Rose, with her appreciation of Art, would say to this.) Later we adjourn to drawing-room—fire now a mere ember—and Lady M. explains that she is not going to the Meeting, but Vice-President will look after me, and she hopes

I shall enjoy Recitation Competition—
some of our members really very clever, and
one in particular, so amusing in dialect. I
nod and smile, and continue to shiver, and
presently car fetches me away to village.
Meeting is held in reading-room, which
seems to me perfect paradise of warmth, and
I place myself as close as possible to large
oil-stove. Vice-President—very large and
expansive in blue—conducts everything
successfully, and I deliver homily about
What Our Children Read, which is kindly
received. After tea—delightfully hot, in
fact scalds me, but I welcome it—Recitation Competition takes place and have to
rivet my attention on successive members,
who mount a little platform and declaim in
turns. We begin with not very successful
rendering of verses hitherto unknown to
me, entitled "Our Institute", and which
turn out to be original composition of
reciter. This followed by "Gunga Din"
and very rousing poem about Keeping the
Old Flag Flying. Elderly member then

announces "The Mine" and is very dramatic and impressive, but not wholly intelligible, which I put down to Dialect. Finally award first place to "The Old Flag", and second to "The Mine", and present prizes. Am unfortunately inspired to observe that dialect poems are always so interesting, and it then turns out that "The Mine" wasn't in dialect at all. However, too late to do anything about it.

Meeting is prolonged, for which I am thankful, but finally can no longer defer returning to arctic regions of Crimpington Hall. Lady M. and I spend evening cowering over grate, and exchanging isolated remarks, and many nods and smiles, across ear-trumpet. Finally I get into enormous four-poster, covered by very inadequate supply of blankets, and clutching insufficiently heated hot-water bottle.

October 5th.—Develop really severe cold twenty-four hours after reaching home. Robert says that all Institutes are probably full of germs—which is both unjust and ridiculous.

October 13th.—Continued cold and cough keep me in house, and make me unpopular with Robert, Cook, and Gladys— the latter of whom both catch my complaint. Mademoiselle keeps Vicky away, but is sympathetic, and brings Vicky to gesticulate dramatically at me from outside the drawing-room window, as though I had the plague. Gradually this state of affairs subsides, my daily quota of pocket-handkerchiefs returns to the normal, and Vapex, cinnamon, camphorated oil, and jar of cold cream all go back to medicine-cupboard in bathroom once more.

Unknown benefactor sends me copy of new Literary Review, which seems to be full of personal remarks from well-known writers about other well-known writers. This perhaps more amusing to themselves than to average reader. Moreover, competitions most alarmingly literary, and I return with immense relief to old friend *Time and Tide*.

October 17th.—Surprising invitation to evening party—Dancing, 9.30—at Lady B.'s. Cannot possibly refuse, as Robert has been told to make himself useful there in various ways; moreover, entire neighbourhood is evidently being polished off, and see no object in raising question as to whether we have, or have not, received invitation. Decide to get new dress, but must have it made locally, owing to rather sharply worded enquiry from London shop which has the privilege of serving me, as to whether I have not overlooked overdue portion of account? (Far from overlooking it, have actually been kept awake by it at night.) Proceed to Plymouth, and get very attractive black taffeta, with little pink and blue posies scattered over it. Mademoiselle removes, and washes, Honiton lace from old purple velvet every-night tea-gown, and assures me that it will be *gentil à croquer* on new taffeta. Also buy new pair black evening-shoes, but shall wear them every evening for at least an hour in order to ensure reasonable comfort at party.

Am able to congratulate myself that great-aunt's diamond ring, for once, is at home when needed.

Robert rather shatteringly remarks that he believes the dancing is only for the *young* people, and I heatedly enquire how line of demarcation is to be laid down? Should certainly not dream of accepting ruling from Lady B. on any such delicate question. Robert merely repeats that only the young will be *expected* to dance, and we drop the subject, and I enquire into nature of refreshments to be expected at party, as half-past nine seems to me singularly inhospitable hour, involving no regular meal whatever. Robert begs that I will order dinner at home exactly as usual, and make it as substantial as possible, so as to give him every chance of keeping awake at party, and I agree that this would indeed appear desirable.

October 19*th.*—Rumour that Lady B.'s party is to be in Fancy Dress throws entire neighbourhood into consternation. Our Vicar's wife comes down on gardener's wife's bicycle — borrowed, she says, for greater speed and urgency—and explains that, in her position, she does not think that fancy dress would do at all—unless perhaps *poudré*, which, she asserts, is different, but takes ages to brush out afterwards. She asks what I am going to do, but am quite unable to enlighten her, as black taffeta already completed. Mademoiselle, at this, intervenes, and declares that black taffeta can be transformed by a touch into Dresden China Shepherdess *à ravir*. Am obliged to beg her not to be ridiculous, nor attempt to make me so, and she then insanely suggests turning black taffeta into costume for (*a*) Mary Queen of Scots, (*b*) Mme. de Pompadour, (*c*) Cleopatra.

I desire her to take Vicky for a walk; she is *blessée*, and much time is spent in restoring her to calm.

Our Vicar's wife—who has meantime been walking up and down drawing-room in state of stress and agitation—says What about asking somebody else? What about the Kellways? Why not ring them up?

We immediately do so, and are light-heartedly told by Mary Kellway that it *is* Fancy Dress, and she is going to wear her Russian Peasant costume—absolutely genuine, brought by sailor cousin from Moscow long years ago—but if in difficulties, can she lend me anything? Reply incoherently to this kind offer, as our Vicar's wife, now in uncontrollable agitation, makes it impossible for me to collect my thoughts. Chaos prevails, when Robert enters, is frenziedly appealed to by our Vicar's wife, and says Oh, didn't he say so? one or two people *have* had "Fancy Dress" put on invitation cards, as Lady B.'s own house-party intends to dress up, but no such suggestion has been made to majority of guests.

Our Vicar's wife and I agree at some length that, really, nobody in this world *but*

Lady B. would behave like this, and we have very good minds not to go near her party. Robert and I then arrange to take our Vicar and his wife with us in car to party, she is grateful, and goes.

October 23rd.—Party takes place. Black taffeta and Honiton lace look charming and am not dissatisfied with general appearance, after extracting two quite unmistakable grey hairs. Vicky goes so far as to say that I look Lovely, but enquires shortly afterwards why old people so often wear black—which discourages me.

Received by Lady B. in magnificent Eastern costume, with pearls dripping all over her, and surrounded by bevy of equally bejewelled friends. She smiles graciously and shakes hands without looking at any of us, and strange fancy crosses my mind that it would be agreeable to bestow on her sudden sharp shaking, and thus compel her to recognise existence of at least one of guests invited to her house. Am obliged, however, to curb this unhallowed impulse, and proceed quietly into vast drawing-room, at one end of which band is performing briskly on platform.

Our Vicar's wife—violet net and garnets —recognises friends, and takes our Vicar away to speak to them. Robert is imperatively summoned by Lady B.—(Is she going to order him to take charge of cloak room, or what?)—and I am greeted by an unpleasant-looking Hamlet, who suddenly turns out to be Miss Pankerton. Why, she asks accusingly, am I not in fancy dress? It would do me all the good in the world to give myself over to the Carnival spirit. It is what I *need*. I make enquiry for Jahsper— should never be surprised to hear that he has come as Ophelia—but Miss P. replies that Jahsper is in Bloomsbury again. Bloomsbury can do nothing without Jahsper. I say, No, I suppose not, in order to avoid hearing any more about either Jahsper or Bloomsbury, and talk to Mary Kellway—who looks nice in Russian Peasant costume—and eventually dance with her husband. We see many of our neighbours, most of them not in fancy dress, and am astounded at unexpected sight of Blenkinsops' Cousin Maud, bounding round the room with short, stout partner, identified by Mary's husband as great hunting man.

Lady B.'s house-party, all in expensive disguises and looking highly superior, dance languidly with one another, and no introductions take place.

It later becomes part of Robert's duty to tell everyone that supper is ready, and we all flock to buffet in dining-room, and are given excellent sandwiches and unidentified form of cup. Lady B.'s expensive-looking house-party nowhere to be seen, and Robert tells me in gloomy aside that he thinks they are in the library, having champagne. I express charitable—and improbable—hope that it may poison them, to which Robert merely replies, Hush, not so loud—but should not be surprised to know that he agrees with me.

Final, and most unexpected, incident of the evening is when I come upon old Mrs. Blenkinsop, all over black jet and wearing martyred expression, sitting in large armchair underneath platform, and exactly below energetic saxophone. She evidently has not the least idea how to account for her presence there, and saxophone prevents conversation, but can distinguish something about Maud, and not getting between young things and their pleasure, and reference to old Mrs. B. not having very much longer to spend amongst us. I smile and nod my head, then feel that this may look unsympathetic, so frown and shake it, and am invited to dance by male Frobisher—who talks about old furniture and birds. House-party reappear, carrying balloons, which they distribute like buns at a School-feast, and party proceeds until midnight.

Band then bursts into Auld Lang Syne and Lady B. screams Come along, Come along, and all are directed to form a circle. Singular mêlée ensues, and I see old Mrs.

Blenkinsop swept from armchair and clutching our Vicar with one hand and unknown young gentleman with the other. Our Vicar's wife is holding hands with Miss Pankerton—whom she cannot endure—and looks distraught, and Robert is seized upon by massive stranger in scarlet, and Cousin Maud. Am horrified to realise that I am myself on one side clasping hand of particularly offensive young male specimen of house-party, and on the other that of Lady B. We all shuffle round to well-known strains, and sing For *Ole* Lang Syne, For *Ole* Lang Syne, over and over again, since no one appears to know any other words, and relief is general when this exercise is brought to a close.

Lady B., evidently fearing that we shall none of us know when she has had enough of us, then directs band to play National Anthem, which is done, and she receives our thanks and farewells.

Go home, and on looking at myself in the glass am much struck with undeniable fact that at the end of a party I do not look nearly as nice as I did at the beginning. Should like to think that this applies to every woman, but am not sure—and anyway, this thought ungenerous—like so many others.

Robert says, Why don't I get into Bed? I say, Because I am writing my Diary. Robert replies, kindly, but quite definitely, that In his opinion, That is Waste of Time.

I get into bed, and am confronted by Query: Can Robert be right?

Can only leave reply to Posterity.

THE END